Pharmakon 6

Cheryl Kvalvik

Dedication

This book is dedicated to Hosea and his ability to see into the future

Contents

Introduction

September 9, 2039

We would have looked funny twenty years ago, three gowned, nun-like figures huddling together and peering through the glass of a hospital nursery window like women who are past their prime and are wishing for another chance. It would have been funny, but today it was serious. North Carolina's Saint Luke's Hospital hasn't seen a baby in ten years. What maternity ward would they go to? People avoid hospitals like the plague to avoid getting the plague. They are focusing desperately on trying to cope with the pounding, stabbing, achy pain. I'm sure having babies isn't even being considered. How many are in pain? No one seems to know.

It was eight years ago when the government made edicts that kept us from seeing each other's faces. Stopping the disease from spreading was the initial goal, but it became important to keep society on equal standing; nobody shunned, excluded or demeaned, the handsome and beautiful from being envied. The only way we even have a clue of the progression of the endemic is by the flow of people who dare to come to the ER to find relief.

They reluctantly show us their faces, they cry, they beg; they finally submit. The malformations from the boils and ectropion, the sagging of the lower eyelids that normally only the elderly experience, is shocking. I saw it on a 10-year-old. And why are collagen levels in teenagers that of 60-year-olds?

Our gowns aren't black, but pastel. Rosa's and mine are yellow. I hate the color. One of the hospital managers, Dr. Lil's, is blue. We also look like we belong to a harem with our veil-like masks hanging down to our collarbones. We are work friends; we are our only friends. We eat at work, are driven to our nearby homes by the company bus, and we live alone.

This endemic doesn't affect everyone, only people born in the United States, thus the reason 8.7 million Americans living in other countries were sent home. And that is where the mystery lies. At the age of 13, I made a promise to myself to solve this mystery and become a nurse and researcher. In this journal, now nearly full, I detailed the history of this disaster. I also noted the facts and procedures in an accountant's ledger my dad gave me on my birthday before he died. I wrote the experiments, theories, and the implementation of ridiculous ideas that proved to be a waste of time, a grasping at straws.

The president began his presidency in 2033 by looking to other countries for help. That is when the Pharmakon 6 team, 6 men from 6 different countries were hired. They didn't wear the garb or masks, but they sure came up with everything we have now. We watch them every night at 7:00, it is the only "news" we get. The situation has become unbearable.

Children began being schooled at home as teachers slowly couldn't cover up what they didn't want exposed, and substitute teachers were in short supply. Classes combined and rooms became crowded until students started disappearing. Television, the new education plan implemented when I was in 9th grade, became the Federal Homeschool Association. Each student had a channel for their grade; we watched for 6 hours a day.

Before starting the homeschool program, I spent an hour a day at the library researching what I could. I knew my dad was sick. He hid his face and wore long sleeves all the time. Then computers and media shut down. At the time, I guessed it was to control the dissenters.

White train cars began moving packaged military type food and water to serving stations. We eat them in the hospital lunchroom twice a day. That is when I can visit with Dr. Lil and Rosa, my only link to people as friends, even though I have yet to see their faces.

I am now nearing the end of this 10 year "medical journal." Has it solved any problems? Not at all, a total waste of time. No, but it has kept me sane and kept me company. I won't start another journal after filling up the last few pages of this one. I will pack it up and hide it deeper than just the hidden compartment under the couch cushion. It is full of the sad and sorry past.

Dad died from their experiments. He was given every antibiotic and who knows what else. Why did his health fail so quickly? I have no answers, I probably never will. I was going to be the one who finally found 'it' under a microscope, and then with an eyedropper full of the perfect solution, douse and destroy the thing. I would have been the hero. Hah, now it seems all I do is prescribe pain pills. What has my research hospital accomplished? Nothing, yes, I will hide this carefully, and maybe someday, someone will find the cure.

Chapter 1

The baby had no deformities, no flaws; a perfect child, 8 lbs. 2 oz. The three figures were so taken by the little one, that when the elevator doors opened, they jumped in surprise. A cameraman with someone holding a microphone froze then quickly closed the elevator doors. Dr. Lil was furious. How did they pass the eye scanner to enter the building? Where was the security? Who would want a film of a baby? "Pharm-6!" she angrily declared. How did this company encroach on so many of their own laws that were set in place to protect privacy? She called security from her com watch and the three rushed to the elevator. The two nurses had never seen their boss this agitated. "We have to protect our patients!" She rushed off and Rosa and Grace started their shift in the ER.

Grace checked patients in and interviewed them, and Rosa was one of the 5 nurses that began treatment. Almost immediately a person in a filthy gown with head down, crept into the empty waiting room and slowly sat down. Grace was used to dealing with the fear of hospitals; it was the new widespread phobia. She went over and sat next to the patient. "I can help you; I just need to ask you a few questions." Grace noticed blood spatter on the gown.

"I need pain pills." It was an odd request because the pharmacies now dispensed them as over-the-counter drugs. Unless she was young.

"How old are you?"

"13."

"Who is your guardian?"

"I don't have one."

"Let me take you where it is more comfortable." Grace knew she had to be careful, or this one would decide to turn around and escape. When they were secluded in the back office, after getting the girl's address, Grace called Rosa in.

"Please take Cindy to the med bed. She is in a lot of pain." The medical beds looked like tanning beds only the top lids were thinner. The person would lie down on a cushioned pad, the lid would close and a stream of liquid with antiseptics, oils and other unknown substances would flow around the body. It was a quick way of cleansing wounds and alleviating pain. The bath was created by Pharmakon 6, and her hospital was able to purchase two of them. It was the one thing coming out of the company that was much appreciated.

"Cindy, you will like this treatment. We will talk later." Grace motioned to Rosa to call her. It was difficult to give subliminal messages without the use of the face. Grace then called the hospital police.

"Hello, Officer, can you go to this address? I have a bad feeling about this, so don't go alone."

"Sure, I'll grab someone and go right over. Today is a busy day," he continued, "this is already the second call, and it isn't even 9:00." Grace knew what the first call was about; the break-in at the nursery.

Heads are rolling, she thought.

An hour later Grace had three officers walk into the ER waiting room. "Let's go to my office." An extra chair was brought in.

"It looks like Cindy's grandmother has been murdered. Her name is Ida March. Do you have any idea who might have done this? You sent us over there, and I am telling you it was not a pretty picture." At that moment the wrist phone vibrated; it was Rosa.

"Excuse me officers, this call may help. Rosa?"

"Grace, I have never seen worse affects from the virus! I had to peel the robe off her," Rosa's voice was cracking. "She is in the med bed now, but her body is covered with boils, and she has been beaten. She is emaciated from starvation, her face looks like she is 40 not 13, and I think she has done something very bad."

"Rosa, we will talk later, thank you." Grace hung up.

"I think the 13-year-old granddaughter did this, she is being treated now, but I also think she was abused, starved and has one of the worst cases of this plague that we have seen in someone this young. Please, let us help get her comfortable before you question her." They agreed, but one officer stayed to make sure the girl wasn't going to be a runner. After getting new robes for the girl, saving the old ones for evidence, and finding her a private room, Grace set a chair outside for the officer. It was lunchtime.

Rosa, Dr. Lil and Grace had much to talk about during lunch which was difficult. Extra-large tables had been brought in years ago to keep people apart, which made having private conversations difficult. In preparation for eating, they hooked one side of their veils to the opposing side under their slightly lifted face guard. Then they would lean over their food to be able to hear. The Doctor was informed about the girl in room 212. Grace agreed to sit with her until she woke up. Dr. Lil shook her head, "A rough morning indeed. I couldn't find out which security guard let them in, or maybe it was someone else. The camera just shows a white jumpsuit opening the side door. These darn masks, how are we supposed to catch criminals? I received a call from Jane from the nursery. she wants me to come up after lunch. Please no more crises!"

"When does Dr. Hernando get back from his trip to Pharm-6?" asked Grace. The other hospital manager was reporting the hospital's laboratory progress, a requirement to receiving funding from the large government corporation.

"Tonight, boy does he have a lot to come back to," remarked Lil. "I better run up to the nursery. I've lost my appetite." She reattached her veil, picked up her tray and left.

"I would have liked her pudding," Rosa never seemed to get enough food. She couldn't be blamed as portions were small and uninviting. Protein was always plant based; coffee was chicory, and spices eliminated.

"See you on the bus?"

"I hope so. I will see how this situation with Cindy goes. I'm hoping she will talk to me."

The two went their separate ways. Grace called in someone to take over for her in the ER and she headed to the elevator. The door opened and Dr. Lil stood there, motioned her in and pushed the basement floor button. Under the un-tinted face guard her eyes were wide open in astonishment.

"Someone in the lab took 4 vials of blood from Mary in the middle of the night. I haven't talked to her yet, but I need to know who did this. I bet they did not know that Mary was one of our nurses, and she knows the protocols."

"Is it unusual to take blood postpartum?"

"Yes, there was no need to draw blood, but the white hooded coveralls hid the culprit. Why do we bother with cameras?"

"Ma'am," Grace inserted, "this may be your connection to what happened earlier. The Pharm-6 group were probably told we had a newborn; they may have even heard that the mom was "clean" and then offered our lab tech money for the blood. On the 7:00 news they were making a call for people who were 'clean' to come forward to be tested. No one trusts them; our memories aren't that short, and people are still convinced that this disease is highly contagious. They would never go to a hospital lab no matter how much money is offered to them. The company is desperate, as they have yet to have a breakthrough. All they ever do is manage this thing, never solving the problem." Now Grace was getting angry. The elevation door opened, and the lab techs looked up.

"Is everyone at work today in this department?" Dr. Lil asked sternly.

"Yes, ma'am, except for Stephen, he worked a late shift then left about an hour ago."

"Do any of you know about the blood testing from last night?" They shook their heads.

"Follow me." Lil led Grace to the glassed-in office containing large refrigerators lining one wall. It belonged to the head of the department, Stephen Holt. She unlocked the door with all eyes watching. "The test tubes will have the date and a code on them. There are 4 of them, Grace." They started on opposite ends and began searching. A lab tech made a quick phone call without being seen. "Stephen should know what is happening," he told the co-worker sitting next to him.

"Could this be it?" Grace held up a tray with 4 vials marked CFC with the correct date.

"Clean female with child maybe? Okay, let's go." The doctor now had the evidence. They put the vials back; left the office, and the doctor put a double lock on the door. She had to be the one to unlock it.

"I will give him a call." Dr Lil continued, "I guess you have a patient to visit." They parted and Grace was glad for two things; one, she wasn't a hospital manager and two, she was able to sit with a sleeping patient and think, far away from the drama.

Stephen did not answer the phone and Dr. Lil skipped her ride home. She would eventually walk the three blocks to the thirty-five unit, 500-square-foot Norwegian style apartments built for hospital staff. The housing was free; the waiting list was long. She liked the simple minimal living with zero heating and cooling costs. It was a building that was perfect in every way, if you lived alone.

Back in her office, Dr. Lil paced back and forth until she realized that she was too hungry to think. As she walked down the corridor with head down, she absentmindedly ran into Dr. Hernando. She was so glad that he couldn't see her blushing.

"I am so sorry, Doctor, I was deep in thought. This has been an awful day, and I hate to bombard you, but do you have time right now? I am heading to the cafeteria for a snack; I haven't eaten much today." She knew she was rambling, but she couldn't stop. She had really wanted all the problems to be solved before he had arrived. It was hard being a woman in this field; always feeling she had to prove herself and earn respect. Worrying was something she did a lot of, and now she worried that she would burst into tears. She wished she had her tinted goggles on.

"Please just call me Chris," was his only comment.

After they sat down, he with coffee and she with a bagel, he told her about his day since she needed to eat. He said that it was only his second time to visit the Pharm office and was still impressed. "It sure looks like a well-oiled machine," he remarked blandly.

"Did they like your report?" she asked between bites.

"Hard to tell. They aren't like Americans who like to talk a lot, but they were polite." She blushed again.

"Here was my day." She leaned in and proceeded with Cindy, the break-in, then the story of Stephen, and her theories about Pharm-6 paying, and maybe even bribing him to get the blood. She didn't mention that Grace had helped. She felt like a school-girl at the principal's office. He reached out and put his gloved hand on top of hers.

"These are small problems, Lily, we can deal with this together and get to the bottom of things. I understand your doubts
about the legality of some of Pharmakon's practices. Let's get
a good night's sleep and make plans tomorrow morning. Does
that sound good?" She nodded.

Lil left the building and started walking the three blocks to
her home when Dr. Hernando pulled up, opened the door of his
sports car and cheerfully told her to get in. She obeyed when she
would have preferred to walk, but the door was already open.

"Thank you, but I am only three blocks away."

"I know that, but I thought you would like to ride in my new
old car. It's an Austin-Healey 3000; I bought it at an auction. I
drove it up to DC, and it ran perfectly." Lil didn't know what to
say, she didn't know about cars, and didn't really care, but mostly she was uncomfortable. Human contact wasn't something she
was used to.

"Really nice car. Thank you for the ride." She pried herself
out of the tiny sports car and waved. "How embarrassing," she
muttered to herself.

Chris Hernando was an all-American guy who always set
high goals for himself. He dove into his work, and his positive attitude is what kept him going. His wife had passed away
from cancer five years ago; his job kept him from dwelling on
the past. His two grown and married sons lived in Texas and
in Arizona and were doing well. One was a veterinarian, and
the other was finishing university to become an anesthesiolo-
gist. He hoped soon to take his new car on a road trip to visit

his boys, their wives and his three grandchildren he had yet to meet.

At home he opened the hospital files and looked up Lily Ann Hollister. "One is always curious about what is behind the mask," he chuckled. There she was, auburn hair, green eyes. "What is the name of that actress that played beside John Wayne, Maureen O'Hare, or was it O'Hara? That's who she looks like." He was genuinely impressed.

Five miles away Dr. Lily Ann Hollister was looking at hospital files on her computer and looking at a 15-year-old picture of Dr. Christian Hernando. "Not too bad, not what I expected. Maybe a cross between Antonio Banderas and Dr. Who." She smiled and read his profile. "Military doctor for five years then private practice. Mother: Ann Sweeny, Father: Jose Hernando who immigrated from Argentina in 1984." She read on until she read the obituary at the bottom about his wife, Elizabeth Aurora. She shut off the computer and felt sad, sad for him and sad that she wasn't better at being comfortable around people. She dreamed that night about running away from cameramen with a baby in her arms.

Chapter 2

Pharmakon 6, in the heart of Washington DC, was a government funded operation and completely autonomous. It did not answer to anyone except for the chief scientist Dr. Marcus Orillion. After a world-wide search for the best possible person to be the new medical leader of the country, he was contacted by the White House. Professor Marcus PHD was most famous in Rome where he trained doctors in modern medical procedures. Italy was reluctant to part with him but understood the draw of the very large salary and the freedom to hire his own team. His move was easy, no family, no deep roots, and a minimalist who was always ready for adventure. His greatest skill was leadership. His first speech to congress was frankly the most uplifting thing they had heard in 3 years. He had a specific plan of attack and was ready with a list of 5 experts who would manage the various departments. Congress hardly glanced at it, voted, and approved it unanimously.

The pharmacy branch, headed by Chinese Dr. Lu, focused on pain and getting rid of old pain management drugs, then began using even older ones. Many men in their 30's were having heart attacks from overdoses of THC, so that became outlawed under the new system. Plus, CBD oil blocked the liver from processing other drugs, so pain killers weren't working. Percocet and Percodan were mass produced. No one feared addiction; the goal was to kill the pain. Soon the pharmacies around the country sold over the counter painkillers to anyone 18 and older. They were given a 30-day supply and could not return to any drug store to buy more until the 30 days were over. It stopped the black-market sales as most people buying them needed them. It did not stop the problem of the long-term use of painkiller creating a need for higher doses.

Another department which worked closely with the pharmacy branch was the research department led by Oxford professor Dr. Bell. There were 15 scientists under his leadership who worked tirelessly to find the cause and cures. The international branch's leader, a Swiss corporate CEO, Alec Schmid, was in charge of the bookkeeping and also kept an ongoing contact with foreign countries. Still, after more than ten years, no other country had been affected. There was an invisible barrier surrounding the United States, no one dared to enter and all foreign born had fled. In the beginning of what they thought was a highly contagious pandemic originating in America, people were given two weeks to flee the country. They had to prove they weren't American born, so their home country would accept them back. The streets emptied of foreign drug smugglers, traffickers and illegal immigrants. They couldn't wait to leave. Bodies were searched to make sure that the people were 'clean'. Fakers were caught and forced to return. Expats in foreign lands were given just weeks to evacuate, or they would face an isolated internment camp with no hopes of ever getting out. Nearly two million Americans, and all 135,000 missionaries were forced to flee. Military planes filled the skies, and every airport in the country took in their returning citizens. The military bases became hospital bases as most of the troops became infected.

A thorough list was made of every difference between the United States and other developed countries. It included the handling of crops, use of fertilizers, poisons and GMOs. Vaccines became suspicious. Additives, and foods banned in Europe and Australia were researched and removed from foods. Drugs that international governments had banned were also categorized and removed from the market. So high was the desperation that congress gave Pharm-6, their nickname, a green light to make all changes deemed necessary. Everything the Pharmakon 6 researched was reported on by their own television news station. America was filled with fear and panic.

People trusted the Pharm-6 company. This put nails in the coffins of other drug companies. No one wanted to take a risk-they were already feeling the bite of this contagion. Farmers with GMO seeds dumped them and ordered seeds from the Pharmakon 6 on-line store that shipped from many other countries. Fields were overturned and virgin farmland was highly sought after. Cattle were again turned onto grassy fields and no GMO corn was used as cow feed. People refused all shots, drugs on the banned list, poisonous cleaners and weed killers. Most people, however, had no energy to do anything except suffer.

The Swedish marketing department head of Pharm-6, Sven Nillson, developed the hooded robes, scrubs, coveralls, masks, veils, foot coverings and goggles. All people had to don their virus/bacteria resistant garb made with copper and other agents that destroyed microbes. Every week hospital robes were cleaned and sprayed with an anti-bacterial and fungal solution. The voice of the crisis, the last department, was public relations lead by Pierre Dupont. They put together the news reports that lasted an hour every night except Sunday. They reported on their accomplishments and findings. The first reports were on how the different colored robes depicted rank, blue being top managers, dark blue were the officers of the law, purple was the president, and so on. Each robe had an engraved RFID code behind the sewn-on name tag of the employee. Eye recognition became the second most important move as faces no longer mattered. Scanning machines on every building read the name and the eye at the same time to allow entry. Certain doors were for those who weren't employees, these were heavily screened with x-ray machines.

The last news report was exceptionally good. The death rate in America had dropped to an historic low. Heart attacks were down, crime down by 80%, cancer and strokes down by half. The only thing that had gone up, and by 60%, was suicides. People did logically figure out that drugs weren't crossing the border, people weren't driving as much, and the sin tax for alcohol, cigarettes and sugar matched that of Norway's. This discouraged smoking, ending much of the death caused by tobacco. Alcohol was heavily monitored similar to the painkillers. Pharm-6 emphasized the four pillars of procedure: control, early treatments, late treatments and seclusion of the infected. Some were leery of the leadership of these foreign entities, and none more that Grace Lynn Iverson. "There has been no control, no treatments, and no vaccines." She mumbled then shut off the TV.

Grace threw off her coverings, as was her daily ritual, and in shorts and a tee shirt made a cup of green tea. She pulled out her ledger and ran her fingers over the cover. In her own 13-year-old writing; it had 2026 on the cover. She picked up a pen and added -2039. The ledger was just for information, facts, dates of discovery, questions and news announcements.

9/10/39: A perfect newborn. Question: Do infected mothers pass it to their unborn child? Was Mary infected?

She put the book away and laid her head back. Seeing Mary's baby was harder than dealing with Cindy. Her discouragement level was still high, and she realized that seeing the infant triggered a deep yearning that her analytical mind and stoic personality was usually able to ignore. That night her dream was of melting faces and painful boils, cries and screams in distant corridors; then a face appeared, a happy smiling face. It looked like her brother Greg, whom she hadn't seen in ten years. She woke with a start and thought of him living in San Francisco, and suffering.

The bus was right on time, 5:20. Grace's stop was the last one. Her house wasn't on the bus route, but since it was only three blocks further than the hospital apartments, they made an exception for her. She paid for the small two-bedroom, one-story place with the settlement money she received from the death

15

of her father. Normally, insurance companies do not pay out for experimental drugs trials, but in this case, since all twenty people died within three days of each other, the court ruled in their favor. The money also covered the remaining cost of her RN degree. She climbed aboard the bus and sat next to Rosa in their regular front row seat. They liked being the first off to be first in line for the eye scanner.

"Where's the boss?" she asked.

"I'm assuming she wanted a head start on the terrible day of dealing with the terrible problems from yesterday. At least Dr. Chris is here to help. I do not like confrontations." Rosa fiddled with her mask.

"You act like it is your conflict, Rosa." Grace smiled, but of course it couldn't be seen. "I have to go first thing to see Cindy. Say a prayer for me please." Grace had never talked like this before, but she felt like Cindy was a bigger problem than the lab selling blood.

"I will." Rosa responded. After being scanned and having their bags searched, they headed for the emergency room.

Chapter 3

The weekly meeting at the round table on the 23rd floor office of the Pharmakon 6 group was ready to begin. Dr. Orillion sat down which signaled that the others could also sit. The Swiss, Schmid, doubled as the secretary and took notes. It was a very non-American group. All wore expensive black suits and had shiny shoes. Most had black hair with some gray around the edges. Dr. Orillion began, "We need to monitor the amount of fear the American people are allowed to experience. We cannot tell them everything. Their fully robed bodies will hide what is happening to their skin."

"I agree, this is true," remarked Pierre Dupont, "but we want to avoid more suicides. We must talk about the saggy eye and skin symptoms, which we became aware of three years ago. Not knowing what is happening to them alone can cause panic. Let's consider hosting a two-week course for surgeons to have them all trained in plastic surgeries. We then can bring them here to operate on volunteers who want a free procedure."

"I am in favor of that idea; we can train nurses also to do Botox, fillers, and scar removal derma abrasion methods. Seeing faces again is our priority. We must get media and Hollywood stars back to work. That will calm the people faster than anything. They need their television and their movie screens to remove the focus on pain. This may also distract those who are suicidal." Dr. Orillion stated, then continued.

"Nillson, I want the government to fund a free, no, three free television stations; one with old movies, one for sitcoms, and one for series shows. The kids have their own channels, so they do not need more." Sven Nillson, hired from Sweden, was the liaison between the president and the company. He took notes and nodded his head. "Pierre, I want a phone bank set up, with as many phones as we can get for people to start making appointments for their face procedures. We will open here, in New York and in California first. Come up with a cost, not too much but enough that we aren't flooded with work. We want all doctors who already have this skill to be recruited regardless of how they are feeling. Offer them whatever they want. And can't we find some popular news people that we can fix up quickly and have them report nonsense to make the people happy?"

"Oui, monsieur," was the answer.

"Begin the implementation of your plan, Pierre, it is a good one. Now let's talk about the election. It is less than two months away, and we are quickly moving forward on many of our public policies before the new administration arrives. Pierre, how is it looking?"

"It looks like our man is a shoe in, he still seems in too much pain to be able to monitor us or push his own game plan. His running mate is a problem though. She is coming out against government control and made a statement that sounded very much like she wants the borders between states to open up again."

Dr. Orillion dismissed the group, "Dupont, stay here for a moment." After the room emptied, he continued, "I want you to do something about the vice president, but make sure it is after the election."

"Yes, sir."

Inside the now empty office, Janitor Joe came in and polished the table, emptied the trash can, and vacuumed. He was an elderly man who was largely ignored. He wore the white scrubs of the service workers and seemed uninterested in science or health. He was indeed interested. He kept every piece of trash, and he listened behind the door of every meeting. He had never trusted these people. His community in the black part of town weren't sick. He didn't see anyone with the signs of this plague. He was happy that the gangs disappeared, and the crime seemed to end, but he did not believe this group of foreigners.

Joe received a radical newspaper, and he hosted meetings where quiet discussions covered each news story. He had friends with CB radios, and one with a ham radio that could get communications to the publisher of the paper. Mr. Joe passed on every bit of info he could find and there was a lot. He would be pleased when he would read his own reports in the paper. These six people ruling the country didn't think the janitor had ears, but he did. He was not able, unfortunately, to listen to the last orders given by Dr. Orillion to his public relations man.

The five heads of the corporation worked long hours to complete their assignments with Marcus Orillion personally taking up the task of implementing higher security measures. A call to the Chinese Secretary of State started the ball rolling on hiring forces to help keep order in areas of the United States that weren't so compliant and were starting to become a danger to the health and well-being of its citizens. Government planes which were the only ones given permission to cross international lines were ready at a moment's notice to begin the transfer of troops. That was one news report that would not show up on the nightly news. Unfortunately, or fortunately, the janitor happened to be washing windows next to the office where that phone call was being made. Doctor Marcus's loud commanding voice, especially when calling long distance, made eavesdropping a cinch.

The weekly secretive neighborhood meeting became somber after Mr. Joe relayed the information about Chinese troops coming to the United States to keep order. "We must not give up hope; we cannot quit now." Joe continued narrating the rest of the plans of the Pharmakon 6. The group's ten members trusted George, and a few other CBers, with the task of sending the coded messages through the information pipeline to Herb, the ham radio expert, who did the long-distance work. They ended with prayer and a song.

Chapter 4

"Knock, knock, Cindy, are you awake?" Grace slowly opened the door after nodding to the officer who was trying not to nod off. She asked him to stand near the slightly ajar door to take any notes he may hear from the conversation. It was important to have someone confirm what she suspected. After seeing that the girl was still sound asleep, she lifted the sheet slightly to see the condition of her back and gasped. There were deep bruises and old scars covering the thin body. She snapped a picture. Cindy stirred and opened her eyes

"I wish I were dead!" she muttered. "I'm going to jail, aren't I?"

"Not if I can help it, Cindy. Why are there scars on your back. I need you to tell me what happened."

"My parents were born in Romania, and both of their families immigrated to the United States. They met in New York and had me. When this disease began, they had to go back to Romania, so they left me with my step grandmother." She covered her face with the sheet and started crying. "She was nice for a few years then overnight she became a tyrant. She beat me, starved me and was so angry that my parents had left me with her. I was afraid. She locked me in my room, and for days I wasn't given any food. Then, I started getting these sores on my body. Every day they got worse. Then my skin got old looking; my eyes turned red and droopy." She ended her story.

Grace knelt beside the bed and quietly whispered into the girl's ear things she hadn't thought of in ten years. "God loves you, Cindy. He cares about you and if you ask, he will forgive you, and then you can forgive yourself. Do you want to do that?"

Cindy nodded from under the sheet.

"Repeat this after me, 'Forgive me God in Jesus' name for hating my grandmother and for letting bitterness enter my heart. Wash away the sin of murder and everything else that doesn't please you. Make me better. I will serve you. Amen."

The weeping continued for 15 minutes, then the child fell asleep. Grace relayed everything that she suspected to the officer, and filled in facts that he hadn't quite heard. His eyes were misting over.

"I am going to order a full autopsy, because it is possible that the grandmother had a health issue or dementia," added Grace.

"Where will she go after this?" he inquired.

"Foster care I imagine. I wish I could come up with a better idea." Grace shook her head.

"I'll take her, I mean, my wife and I will. We can't have children, and this girl needs a healthy home. I can't let anything else happen to her." The policeman was touched by this tragic story.

22

"I will look into this for you, thank you for caring." Grace put her hand on his shoulder, her eyes were now misting up.

"Cindy, I am going to go now. How do you feel?"

"Better, but tired."

"You get some sleep, everything is going to turn out, I promise." She hoped with all her heart that she could keep that promise. She walked by the nurse's station and told them to make sure the girl in room 212 received large portions of food, "She's been starved for many months."

Lunch was just the two nurses. Rosa was so relieved that Cindy was better.

"Dr. Lil is having lunch with Dr. Chris, in his office!" Rosa whispered

"I'm sure they are talking about Stephen and how to deal with the Pharm issue. Yesterday was full of debacles." Grace wasn't much for gossip.

"What is a debacle?" Rosa was a nurse borrowed from Mexico and was still learning English words.

"Major problem or fiasco. Like in our case, a series of unfortunate events."

The bus ride home was quiet. Dr. Lil wasn't with them, so they didn't find out about the lab issue. "Rosa, I don't know when I have been so tired and disturbed. I feel like I am at the end of my rope. Sorry, this was an emotional day, which I am not used to having."

"It's okay, you need to go for a walk when you get home. Get some fresh air and enjoy what's left of the autumn sunshine."

Grace nodded, and after getting off the bus she walked to the park only three blocks from her house. She had never gone there before; had never even taken a walk. A bench sat under a tree on a knoll overlooking a small lake in the distance. There were people walking around the lake. She started counting them. Then stopped, they weren't wearing coverings! She quickly looked around to check for police, then realized that the cops would never care about people walking around a lake, plus they weren't in sight of the road. A perfect hideout for uncloaked health nuts. She began counting again and reached 20, when someone sat down next to her. She jumped.

"I'm sorry I startled you." She glanced at the totally uncovered, unmasked man next to her and wanted to run.

"You are quite uncovered!" She was horrified because it just wasn't done, ever, at least not in her world.

"And you look a bit like my grade school nun teachers. Although they wore black. I like this color. Oh, and I'm immune. I can't give anything to you, and obviously you can't give anything to me. I see that you work in the hospital, Saint Luke's?" She nodded. "Nice to meet you, I am Jonathan Friedman, and you are sitting on my bench." He said in a matter-of-fact sort of way.

Grace was stunned. "I didn't know this was your bench, I thought this was a public park?" She began to get up.

Jonathan laughed and pulled her back down. "I was just joking. I only meant that I try to come here every day after work to have some quiet reflective moments."

"I'm disturbing you then, I better let you reflect." She sounded snarky but didn't care. He was forward and rude.

"By reflective, what I really mean is lonely, and I would like a bit of company if you don't mind. I am a newspaper editor, printer and writer. I live in the Jewish section of town 3 miles east. I jog here, sit, then jog back. It keeps me from having a heart attack."

"What? You don't look like you're 30 years old. You are already worrying about a heart attack?" She turned to get a better look at him.

"Not worried, but sedentary jobs need to be balanced with exercise. My father and grandfather both died at 52 from heart attacks, as a tailor and an accountant, they both were very sedentary."

"My parents were both accountants. My mom for a florist shop, and my dad was a CPA. So how old are you?"

Jonathan smiled, "I am 28, but never too early to care about the health. Let me guess about you. You are 63 years old, contemplating retirement, especially after this particularly rough day at the office. You have stylish short grey hair, and you've kept your youthful figure, which everyone has, as we are all eating those skimpy rations." He belted out a laughter that startled her further.

"Well, you did get some of the facts correct, but I won't tell you which ones. You are the first person I have heard laugh in, well, years. It was a little scary." She rose to leave.

"Let me walk you home; make sure you're safe."

"I am not sure that you are safe."

"I am just trying to be kind to this dear old lady that hasn't seen flesh and blood, well, you probably have seen plenty flesh and blood, but not the healthy kind, right?"

"Promise you are not a stalker?" she retorted gruffly.

"I promise, plus I prefer woman my age, so you have nothing to worry about. Tell me about your job."

Grace proceeded to share generalities, managed to keep her cool until she said good-bye and shut the door. *What is wrong with you, Grace, you freak out about being around a human being and having a normal conversation.* She plopped down on the couch and reviewed every bit of the conversation. *He thinks I'm in my 60's. He was joking probably. He was overly happy and free with his words. Maybe that is what normal is? He is quite handsome, but Jewish so he wouldn't be interested in me.* She had a hard time going to sleep on the one night she needed it the most. Her dreams were of her laughing brother with lots of black curly hair and dark eyes.

The next morning, she sat by Rosa, told her about the guy she met and how awkward and frightening it was. Rosa laughed and told her to loosen up, then whispered.

"I want to show you something when we get to work. Let's meet in the main floor bathroom."

Grace was curious; after being scanned she veered off into the restroom. Rosa followed at a distance.

"What is it, Rosa?"

"Come here, quick." She motioned for her to enter the extra-large disability stall, then shut the door.

"SHHH," Rosa then ripped off her veil and hood. Thick, black hair fell over her shoulders. Her round face and beautiful smile were stunning. Grace then compulsively pulled hers off, and a ponytail of curls was exposed. They stifled their giggles and redressed.

"How old are you, Rosa?"

"Thirty, and you?"

"Twenty-six."

"Boss is 42, I looked her up."

"Rosa, you shouldn't," and they burst into laughter. The restroom door opened, and Rosa hopped up onto the toilet. Grace slipped out, then Rosa followed after the intruder left.

A note on Grace's desk summoned her to Dr. Lil's office. She was always nervous when this happened thinking she was in trouble. Maybe cameras caught them in the bathroom? She flashed back to 8th grade when she started sneaking off to the library to do research on the new plague. The PE class had grown so large that the teacher quit taking role. Grace was caught one time. The principal asked where she was going, and she had answered honestly.

"I'm going to the library to find out more about this thing that is making my dad and all these teachers sick."

"Very well then, be careful when crossing the streets. And do your parents have a problem with you leaving school early?"

"I can't tell them. They are trying to protect me, but it makes me scared. They won't even let me watch the news, and the computer is off-limits." If she had been the type to cry, she would have.

"If your parents get mad at you for this, do not tell them that I gave you permission. Got it?"

"Yes, sir. You are not giving me permission to do this today or every day that I have PE where all we do is jumping jacks, push-ups, and watch stupid movies about sports rules and how to eat healthy food." It felt good to give him her opinion.

"I understand. You are dismissed."

From that day on, until the school closed, she took copious notes from the hour allowed on the computers at the public library. She researched words like boils, pandemic, immigration, deportation, infection, and read news articles until she was sure she knew as much as anyone about what was happening. On her 13th birthday, after her mom gave her the extra-large journal and the huge ledger, she transferred all the details she learned into these two books and promised herself that someday she would find a solution. She now thought of her mom's words as she was unwrapping her gifts.

"I hope you like these. I found them in your dad's desk drawer, and he said you could have them. The pens, pencils, and highlighters are from him too." Her mom seemed worried that she would not like the gifts.

"Mom, they are perfect. I love them! And Mom, I am going to be a nurse and maybe a doctor when I grow up."

Chapter 5

Dr. Lil motioned for Grace to sit. "Here's the story, and I need your help, well, your support. Stephen admitted to taking Mary's blood without asking, but Dr. Chris and I agree that we can forgive him if Mary can. I think that Chris, Dr. Chris, has seen that Pharm-6 has overstepped their boundaries by pressuring Stephen, and I supposed $30,000 wasn't just tempting, it was their way of buying loyalty. We all know what happens if we are not viewed as loyal. This is between us, right?" Grace nodded.

"This is the plan. You will join Stephen and I on the third floor in twenty minutes. Mary is getting ready to be discharged, and we are going to try to appease her with apologies and bribes if needed."

Grace's heart started racing. "Bribes?"

"No, I mean compensations. Any other questions?"

"Why must I be there?"

"You are more of a peer to Mary, and having Stephen there, a man, and me, her boss, without someone she can relate to, might be intimidating for her." Grace nodded.

They met in the waiting room in the empty maternity wing.

"I will go see if she is ready." At that moment Mary, being pushed in a wheelchair, came around the corner. Her face and hair were uncovered, and in her arms was the infant.

"What did you name her?" blurted out Grace.

"Mercy." They all stood there silently. Stephen's conscience was getting the best of him, he couldn't take his eyes off the child. Grace was enjoying looked at Mary's beautiful face, and Dr. Lil wondered how to proceed.

"Let's sit down," announced Dr. Lil, and in unison they sat.

"Stephen, I would like you to begin." Stephen stood up and cleared his throat.

"I apologize with all my heart, and not just because I was caught, for taking your blood without permission. I was offered $30,000 for it. As you know, the Pharmakon company is struggling to get uninfected blood to experiment with. I had heard the rumor that you were 'clean', and I reported that to the company. They did not tell me to get it illegally, so I take full responsibility, and I will do anything you ask of me so I can make this right. Please will you have mercy on me and forgive me?"

Mary started chuckling then laughed, Grace caught on and finally Lil.

"Stephen, how could I hold this against you when you use my own daughter's name in your defense. I don't even think you planned that. Of course, I forgive you. And there is only one thing I ask, no two. First, no name on the blood, it's yours, and I am sure the lab needs the money. And second, I would like you all to come to my house for dinner in two weeks on Tuesday night at 6:00. I would also like discussing this plague with you. Sound good?"

"Thank you!" was all that Stephen could utter, he was so relieved he nearly fainted and had to sit back down.

"We will be there, thank you so much for being understanding, and we are looking forward to dinner. Can we bring anything?" Having three people over during a time of food shortage was unheard of.

"Oh, no. just bring a notebook and pen in case you want to take notes." At that, the nurse had Mary cover her face and head, then she pushed her to the elevator.

"I don't know when I have been so relieved. Your speech was the best apology speech I have ever heard. As far as I'm concerned, you are forgiven, Stephen." The Doctor added.

"Do you think she wants us to come to her house uncovered?" Grace wondered aloud.

The ride home, after dropping Dr. Lil off, was hilarious. Grace and Rosa couldn't help giggling at the story of Stephen's apology. Grace made Rosa promise not to tell anyone the story, "I forgot I was to keep it secret!" Then they giggled about their meeting in the restroom.

"We could be arrested you know." They hadn't laughed so hard in years. Grace thought of Jonathan.

"I wonder if they need nurses in prison?" The laughing caused the bus driver to turn and glance at them. The second stop was at Rosa's hospital owned apartment building. Hers was the older, slightly taller one with higher electric bills.

Grace wanted to relax but also wanted to take a walk. She chose the walk. Jonathan was there.

"Are you waiting for me?" She quickly realized that a 60-year-old woman would not say such a flirtatious thing. She blushed; sometimes masks were helpful.

"I brought you something, and decided that if you didn't come, I at least know where you live." He had such smiling eyes. She tried not to stare. "How was your day?" He continued.

"It was remarkable." She proceeded to tell the tale of taking off the hoods and masks in the hospital restrooms. "I also did something that I have never done, I prayed for a poor girl with no family who is very ill. There was no hope in her life and my childhood lessons came back to me. It seemed to calm her down. Plus, the cop who was with me said that he and his wife would like to take her in."

"Did you grow up in church?" He asked.

"Yes, until I was 13, my mom took me to the Baptist church down the road. I even went to vacation Bible school every summer."

"Here is the latest edition of my paper." He handed her a rather thin copy, she read the title, "*Zion Herald*, that is an interesting name. Thank you!" He walked her home and said goodbye. She immediately threw off her gown, sat down and opened the newspaper. She went through and read the headings first. *Pole Shifts By 2 Degrees, 20,000 Fireballs enter the Atmosphere, USGS Stops Reporting Earthquakes, Comets Worse than Asteroids, 100 Volcanoes Erupting, Food Supply Chain in Trouble, Ice Caps Melting from Heat of Sun, More Plagues on Horizon.* She read that article. The report talked about the uprising of malaria, dengue fever, and Ebola in different parts of the world. She scanned the rest of the headings; *China has 30,000 Policing Troops Heading to America.* After reading that article she threw the paper down. She was furious, "This is all untrue, can't be true." She felt panic and turned on the 7:00 news. "Surely Pharm-6 will have their regular truth and good positive news!" She was now talking to herself. The company's face, Pierre Dupont, was usually the only reporter.

"Tonight, we will be hearing from our extraordinary leader, Dr. Orillion. It is a special night of great news and encouragement for your magnificent country." His accent was thick and his sing-song voice irritating. "I introduce you to the one who has been given the high honor of this position." He began to clap as Dr. Orillion walked onto the set.

"Thank you, Mr. Dupont." Grace was annoyed that he didn't say he was proud to serve the nation. "He's just plain proud," she mumbled.

"I will quickly get to the main points. We will now have Chinese peacekeepers on American soil able to help with policing the country. The security has grown lax, and new reports of people not abiding by the government's safety laws are pouring in. Soon order will be returned." Grace gasped.

"Next, we have a new training program for doctors, nurses and estheticians who will be able to deal with scarring and face lifts. All doctors will be required to have this training as we will see an influx of people wanting to fix what this endemic has created. We will get your news crews back and your beloved movie stars." Grace stood up and yelled at the television, which was completely out of character, but she could not believe what she was hearing. "Are you hearing this, America?"

"Our need for specialists has diminished because the country has become healthier." He continued, "Heart attacks and cancers have dropped tremendously. Sugar diabetes is the lowest it has been in 50 years. We have much to celebrate." At this point Grace began to cry with frustration, "SOLVE THE REAL PROBLEM!" She nearly shut off the television.

"We will do the training during the winter months and by next spring every hospital and clinic will have a skin care wing. In the meantime, it is time to bundle up as this winter is looking to be extra cold with more than the usual amount of snow and ice. Try to get at least 30 minutes of sun every day for your vitamin D. God bless and have a nice holiday season." The station went to elevator-type music that played until the next night at 7:00.

"How could I have been so blind?" Grace picked up the paper and read every article, then wondered how Jonathan could be so cheerful.

Chapter 6

The next day was cold and rainy, it matched the mood. Grace spoke little on the ride to work. Rosa rattled cheerfully on, and Dr. Lil obviously had other things on her mind. Grace went first thing to visit Cindy, who sat up in bed, and was not hiding her face.

"Good morning sweetheart. I hope you had a good night?" Grace was astonished at how much better she looked. The eyes seemed to be healing, and she could almost see the youth coming through.

"I am going to live with that cop and his wife. A social worker, lawyer and another cop came in this morning and asked lots of questions. They looked at my back and decided that it was self-defense and not murder, and I could be put in foster care instead of prison."

"I don't think they would have put you in prison. But I am so glad, Cindy. It looks like your stats are good. When do you want to go to your new home?"

"Right now!" She exclaimed.

"I will talk to the front desk. And see when Mrs. Foster care mom can come and get you."

"Oh, she is on her way right now."

"Okay then, I will just wait here and meet her when she comes." Ten minutes later, a tan cloaked women came in carrying a dozen balloons and a box of chocolates.

"I will let you two get acquainted while I go talk to the head nurse. Thank you for taking care of Cindy, I've become rather fond of her."

The nurse started the hospital check out procedure, and Grace went to the ER in time to clock in for work. A gnawing fear was growing inside her, and she couldn't shake the feeling of impending doom. Rosa noticed it at lunch. "What is your problem today?"

"It is a very long story. I will bring something for you to read tomorrow. But good news, Cindy is going home today to her new family."

"I hope they are a good family."

"Believe me, I will keep doing follow-up on her. I have the address and will be dropping in. The days are over where we can look at someone to discern whether they are good people or not. I met Mr. Handsome again at the park. He is so cheerful, and I really can't figure out why. There is so much bad going on right now."

Rosa patted her gloved hand, "We keep living and having hope, my friend. Don't give up hope."

"I will try, but things are much worse than I thought. I feel like I have been deceived. Did you watch the news last night with Dr. Nightmare?"

"Rosa chuckled, "I knew all this was coming, I knew it was bad from the start. You in America have lost your freedoms, your luxuries, and have just accepted it. If you want a little hope, then venture out and see how many communities are doing well. Here's a secret, my community doesn't have the disease, and no, most aren't from foreign countries. I know what you're thinking, I am not talking about my apartment building; I am talking about my people that I visit every weekend on the West side. We visit and eat together completely maskless and garbless. We are all healthy. Go investigate other communities. Check out the real world. Working in a hospital makes one fearful and cynical. You are way too young for that. Yes, the truth can be shocking and can hurt, but surely you can see that all aspects of life in America has changed and not all for the bad."

"You are right, Rosa. I am sorry. Have you heard of the *Zion Herald*?"

"Of course, it is passed around all over the place."

"Why didn't you tell me? It is that guy's paper, Jonathan Friedman, the one I met in the park!"

"Wow, that is great! He is doing such an important job. Find out how he gets all his information; I would love to know. Since the blackout of news, media and internet, it has been our only source. I have been very curious about him."

"Sure, I'll ask him if I see him again." Grace was stunned. Her estimation of the man was raised, and she was now sure that he wasn't just spreading falsities. She could not wait for the day to end.

Grace practically trotted to the bench under the leafless tree. The wind was getting colder, and she wondered how she would do this in the dead of winter. *Maybe he stops coming when it's cold.* She waited for half an hour and finally rose to leave. The winter robes were being brought in next week; these were just not warm enough. She walked slowly to the house, but he never came.

At 10:00 she was wakened by pounding on her front door. Her first thought was Chinese peacekeepers. She flung on her robe and peeked through the peephole. It was Jonathan.

"What are you doing here, is everything okay? She forgot he had not yet seen her. Her hair being very curly and long, was wildly sticking out everywhere. "Come in." She could see he was troubled.

"I am sorry to bother you, but I was looking for a much older woman." He then smiled. "My rabbi fell, and I think he broke his arm. He is rather old-fashioned and refuses to go to the clinic or hospital. Can you possibly help me?"

"Do you have a car?"

"Yes."

"Good. I will get dressed, then we can drive to the hospital where I can get supplies, though I would really like an x-ray."

He shook his head. "Sorry, we have to do this the old-fashioned way for my old-fashioned friend."

They walked into the small house to the back bedroom. An elderly man was sitting on the bed holding his arm. He looked up at the nurse in a yellow gown and veil. "You don't look like a nun. Don't they wear black?"

"Yes sir, this is what I have to wear at the hospital, and I had to go there to get supplies." She removed her head coverings and pulled out an injection.

"What is that?" He demanded.

"Sir, I can't handle seeing people in pain. I get enough of that every day. I can't touch you unless you are more comfortable. I promise this is safe, and it will relax you and allow me to work. I have more in case I have to set the arm. I pray not. But I do have to determine the extent of the injury." He agreed, and she gave him the shot.

"Tell me exactly how this happened."

"I got up to use the bathroom, tripped on the rug and slammed into the doorway." She could see he was slowly relaxing, and she carefully felt his arm. A tear left his eye, and she knew this would be a rough night.

After determining that the bones were not displaced; she wrapped a plaster cast around his arm, gave him another shot and left pain pills for him to take. She arrived home at 1:00 A.M.

"I owe you one," smiled Jonathan. "I'm afraid now that I know you aren't 62, I might be stalking you."

"Sixty-three, remember? Can you come in; I need to ask you something. Want a cup of tea?"

"No, thank you on the tea. I hope to get a few hours sleep before I start the day." They sat on the couch.

"Rosa, my friend at work, reads your paper. She wanted me to ask you how you get your info."

"Ham radio and CB operators, there is a network of us that not only spans the country, but we have several operators from the pentagon, NASA, and other scientists and astronomers on our network. I knew that the paper would probably be hard to swallow. It is waking up the county though. It would take hours to fill you in on everything." He put his hand on hers. "Thank you again for helping my friend."

"I think I should follow up on him. Can you pick me up on Sunday?"

"Sure, I will be here at 11:00."

"A.M., I hope."

Chapter 7

Dr. Lil couldn't believe what she heard on the nightly news. Without thinking, she called Dr. Chris. "Did you see the news?" she asked rather loudly.

"Who is this?" Dr. Chris knew who it was, he had caller ID on his hospital wrist phone. She knew he knew, but she was flustered. "This is Lil. Did you know all this was coming?"

"Yes, I was informed at the meeting I just attended in DC. It is disturbing, but we will get through it. The training is on-line through our hospital media center. We will have to watch two hours a night for two weeks then we will travel to HQ for practice sessions with the experts in eye surgeries and face lifts for us surgeons. They are coming in from around the country to train us. You and I will both be required to do face lifts."

She was silent for a few seconds. "But I don't want to do that. Can I get out of it?"

"Let's talk about this further. I have a steak that I have been saving. How about Saturday night after I leave work? I can swing by and pick you up at 6:30. Don't give this another thought. It isn't worth worrying about. See you tomorrow."

"Goodbye." She managed to say. *He must think I'm at idiot. I don't need comforting. Can't he see how this is taking over our country? People telling us what we can and cannot say and do. The last thing I want to do is have dinner with him. He didn't even let me say no thank you!"*

In jeans, sweatshirt and her thick auburn hair pulled back to give her a more severe look, Lily glanced at herself in the mirror. She was pale and had a slight rash from an allergic reaction to the veil. She decided a little make-up, and a touch of blush and lipstick wouldn't give him the wrong idea, but she skipped the perfume. She wondered if he would honk. He didn't know her apartment number. She put on her heavy coat and gloves but skipped the gown and the rest of the coverings. She was certain he wouldn't be wearing them at home. She watched through the curtains, and when she saw his car pull up, she left.

He chatted throughout the ride, which was good, because she wasn't in the mood. He talked about the new program which only made her blood boil. She clinched her jaw and her fist. She hadn't felt this angry since they took real coffee out of the cafeteria. The car turned off onto a long driveway with an entrance gate. The car pulled up in front of an estate which reminded Lily of the old colonial homes in Mississippi.

"Beautiful!" She couldn't help saying it.

"Thank you. It has been in the family for three generations of doctors. The first was a veterinarian, who made his wealth on cutting edge animal surgeries. I've been thinking of selling though and putting my name on the list where you live." He unlocked the front door, and they entered a large entryway.

"Beautiful." She repeated. "This mahogany is lovely and rare these days. Why in the world would you give up what, a 5,000 square foot home for a 500 square foot one! Do you even know what it is like feeling caged in? If I had anywhere else to go besides work, maybe it wouldn't be too bad, but no church, no gyms, no theaters! Frankly, I will just trade you. I'm joking of course I know I can be too outspoken. Would you show me the house after dinner?"

"Of course, and you are right, I am being insensitive. I'll go change and be right down. Make yourself comfortable."

He came downstairs wearing jeans and a sweatshirt. It was her first chance at getting a good look at his face. He did look older than his picture, but she thought the 15 years had made him better looking. She studied his black hair sprinkled with gray when his back was turned. He washed his hands. "When my wife passed, sentimentality also died in me. A man's home is his castle, but without a queen, it can be a dungeon. Please sit down at the island while I cook." He took out a lovely, marinated steak, the biggest one she had seen in 20 years.

"Where did you get one that big?"

"About two years ago I bought a steer, and had it butchered for quite a small fortune. Then I bought two freezers for the meat. Unfortunately, it is nearly gone, but I have had my name on a waiting list with a farmer to buy another."

"Is that why you don't eat in the cafeteria?"

The doctor cringed. "That food is horrid. What is it? I admit to living in luxury while others have suffered. I even have real coffee. Want some?" She nodded and was deciding that having this man as a friend may have its rewards. She studied him while he cooked and wondered if he had any scars from face lifts. It was hard not to stare. When was the last time she had an opportunity to study a normal human, let alone a handsome one.

"So, tell me about your wife." She was changing the subject away from food.

"She was Italian; raised in Boston. She was a clean freak and a perfectionist but fun, and she was a great mom to our children. Her picture is over there on the piano." Lily walked over and looked at the beautiful face, and wished she had worn more make-up, used perfume and had worn nicer clothes.

During dinner Lily tried hard not to groan in delight at the delicious meal. Tender steak, mashed potatoes and gravy, fried okra and apple pie; she was feeling very happy.

"The steak was delicious, Dr. Chris, now give me the tour."

"Call me Chris. Up the stairs are four bedrooms. There are two more in the basement." She paused to look at the pictures in the hallway of his boys growing up, and then ones with their families.

"This one is Paul, and this one is Chris Jr." He showed her the rooms quickly and seemed uncomfortable doing so. Then they went into the daylight basement where there was a huge area with a pool table.

"This is big enough for church!" She exclaimed.

"The boys had parties in here and their eagle-eyed mom never left the room." He led her back up the stairs, and she decided not to ask to see the other two bedrooms.

"My office is in there." She went over and peaked in. It was a very large room with shelves of books covering three walls. He walked to the leather couch, sat down and waited for Lily to sit. He then became serious. "I want you to know, between us, that I am not at all in support of Pharm-6 policies, procedures, or the changes they are making. They are ruining out country. Do we even know how many people are sick and in pain? No, because they are covering us up. Lily, I believe that only maybe 30% of the country are infected, and the rest of us are too afraid to remove the masks. I am not going to give in to fear and frustration, but I have seen evidence of the changes that may be coming. We just have to start changing in here." He pointed to his heart. "I have been through the valley of the shadow of death, and I will have no more fear. Want more wine?" Alcohol was something that America had plenty of. Liquor stores had more bottles lining their shelves than the grocery store had food, but people were only allowed one bottle of alcohol a week which was thoroughly monitored. He bought the best. She nodded.

"I think I have misjudged you. I mistook your positive attitude with a submission to the inevitable." She remarked.

"I don't blame you. I have a feeling that everything we say is being monitored. I don't have proof, but that is why I only wear my watch at work," He pulled up his sleeve to show his wrist to emphasize his point. "I tell you what, I will keep the house so you can visit and have some space to move around in. I realized that I do need to share with others to keep from being a pitiful, miserly scrooge who regrets the past and has no hope for the future. Do you play the piano?" She found it interesting at how quickly he changed subjects and how often. She wondered if he had ADD.

She sat at the piano and played a few pieces she had memorized as a teenager. She ran her fingers over the ivory keys and felt the longing to be done with nursing and just sit and play all day. "Then I would be selfish," she said aloud.

"What?"

"Oh, did I say that out loud? I was longing to retire and sit and play the piano all day. I was dreaming. Well, this piano is beautiful; I love grand pianos. I haven't seen one in twenty years or more." She ran her hand over the shiny black finish. "You must have a housekeeper," noticing the lack of dust.

"Yes, I hired a gal that comes in one day a week. I had her come today." He smiled again.

He drove her home, and neither of them spoke. She thought of Daphne du Maurier's novel "Rebecca'" and the mansion called Mandalay, and he thought of when he could arrange their next date.

Everyone noticed Dr. Lil's happy disposition the next day. They thought it was because it was Sunday, the day she only worked for a few hours. Dr. Chris came in also, and it was his day off. She wandered into the cafeteria and spotted him.

"Hi, thank you again for the steak," she whispered the word steak even though no one was around. They laughed.

"Want to come over for lunch? Only hamburgers, but I have pickles."

"Are you a hoarder of food? Are you one of the lucky ones that listened to the warning signs and built a room just for food storage?"

"Want to see it?"

"Sure!"

Chapter 8

"Hi Mom, sorry it's been a while since I've called. So much has happened here, and I am so tired when I get home that I barely have time to drink my tea and watch the news. I know, what do you think about it? Be careful, Mom, our phones may be tapped. Yes, even landlines. I'm going to come see you, and then we can talk. Are you okay? Good. Yes, I can order you some new robes. Pharm-6 has a web store. I will do it right away. News? Well, I met a man. No, don't get excited because he is Jewish, and I don't think they marry us other people. Really? Well, I am not going to tell him that your great-grandmother was an Ashkenazi Jew. I think that would be rather forward. I know, Mom, but I am still young. My boss? She's 42, but I think she may have a boyfriend too. I'll tell you later. I will figure out a way to come see you, as a nurse I can easily get a pass, then I would need to borrow a car. It's $10 a gallon now, but I can pay for it. Love you too." Grace's mother lived by herself in Northern Virginia. She hadn't seen her in over two years, and she was feeling guilty. Her mother had a great community of friends and never complained about anything except for never hearing from her son. Her mom wasn't the type to lay on the guilt trip, but nevertheless, she felt guilty.

Grace pulled out her ledger, opened to the beginning and scanned her old entries. *Not told what is going on. Chartered planes are bringing Americans back. Cartel assisting the police in escorting U.S. citizens across the border (what is a cartel?). Internment camps in operation, (what is an internment camp?). My dad became a guinea pig for the largest drug company in the world. Drug companies lose their government funding. Computer sites are going down. I can't research any longer.* She turned to the back pages and made more entries; *Surgeons will soon be training to do face lifts. Nurses training to be estheticians. Newspaper 'Zion Herald' blew me away!"*

Grace ordered a tan robe for her mother, the appropriate colored winter robe for the unemployed. She had an hour before Jonathan picked her up to check on the rabbi. She ventured out without her garments for the first time; she didn't figure the police would care. She pulled the coat tight around her; the weather had turned and began to look bleak. She was tired of hiding and tired of not having any fun. What was it her dad used to say, "All work and no play makes Jack a dull boy?" She felt dull. She walked down the hill to the lake and walked around it. The elderly were walking, and they weren't wearing masks. She couldn't look them in the eye to study whether they were infected. She promised herself that one day she would. She would hear their stories. Maybe the answers she needed was out here and not in the stuffy hospital. She walked home then sat by the window watching for Jonathan's car.

"Hi, I brought more pain killer in case the rabbi needs it," she offered.

"Thank you, and it's nice to see your face, you are very pretty." He was certainly bold.

"Thanks, so are you." They both laughed. She could be bold too.

Rabbi was happy to see her; they chatted for a while. She handed him the drugs, but he didn't think he would need them. His eyes suddenly had a faraway look, "They feed on the sins of my people and relish their wickedness."

"What feeds on the sins, Rabbi?" She asked, but he had nodded off.

"He does that often. I usually write down things he says, because I think at times they have a deeper meaning. Let's go for a walk." Jonathan led her out to the street. People were walking around and visiting. "Aren't they afraid of the new Chinese police force?" The nagging worry had crept into her heart like biting insects.

"These people are ready to die for their freedom, Grace. They won't give in, and they certainly aren't going to be fearful. Some of these people had great-grandparents in Nazi camps. They have heard the stories, and they will not let it happen again."

"So how do they stop it? With guns?"

"No, they are going to trust God. Do you notice something? Look around, what do you see?"

"No robes, no masks."

"What else?"

"I guess they look happy. Happy hasn't been seen in a long time. It is like a breath of fresh air." With that she took a deep breath.

They drove home in silence. Grace was wrestling with a concept, an idea. Trusting was hard for her. "I want to show you something. Do you have time to come in?"

"Sure," he followed her inside, and she pulled out her ledger and ran her fingers over it. "I started this when I was 13, when I became determined to find out why my dad died. Don't laugh, it may seem like a dumb idea, but anyway, here it is." She handed him the book, and he sat down. He scanned the columns and asked, "What are the red lines, the yellow highlights and the asterisks?"

"The yellow highlights are the changes or laws the government, then Pharm-6 implemented. The red underlines are things that stood out to me; that I had questions about, and the stars are the policies and practices that made no sense at all." Jonathan spent 15 minutes in silence reading parts of the entries. "Grace, I need a big favor from you."

"Okay, what?"

"I need to borrow this book. It has so much information that I could turn into a series for my newspaper. Now hear me out. I haven't had this much background, and I think it could be called, *A History of the Endemic,* a perfect title for an educational piece that would allow the people to have broader view of what we are dealing with. This is astounding!"

"You had me with educational. There is nothing more satisfying than to have someone appreciate one's writings. I feel like my life hasn't been such a waste."

"Not a waste at all, and I think you may still find a solution to our painful dilemma. Plus, I think you would be surprised at how many people will end up seeing this history." He grabbed her shoulders, sad goodbye and rushed out of the house yelling, "Goodbye, see you later, and thanks again."

Grace felt funny; like she had just lost something and found something at the same time. She realized that her writing in that ledger for so many years had become a habit; she also realized that maybe it wasn't such a foolish endeavor after all.

Sunday was sunny but cold. The new winter gowns had arrived the day before, and Dr. Lily was able to pick hers up at the hospital gown dispensary. Each week the nurses and doctors would pick up a clean uniform and turn in the soiled one which would be taken to a high-tech laundry service that cleaned and sorted the gowns, veils and head coverings. At the beginning of summer two cooler uniforms were handed out and at the beginning of winter, two warmer ones. "I would have liked yellow instead," thought Dr. Lil.

On this meeting with Dr. Chris (she would not call it a date), she wore a long light green angora sweater with brown leggings. She used mascara, eye liner, foundation, blush and eye shadow. She removed the eye shadow. She wore her hair high in a free style bun showing off the curls that she let escape from the hair tie. She slipped on her favorite brown leather coat that she hadn't worn in years and then decided against jewelry. At the end she used only a drop of perfume and hoped he wouldn't notice. Her heart was in her throat. "Why am I so nervous!"

She forgot her hospital phone watch and ran to the bedroom to retrieve it when there was a knock on the door.

"Hi, Lily, I was wondering if I could peek at your apartment. In case we decide to trade places?"

"Come in. Here is the kitchen, living room, the dining table, and back here is the bedroom and the bathroom." She loved that he called her Lily. She had never liked 'Lil', but it sounded more professional. Lil was what they called her in college; she was tired of it.

"Very cozy! I watched a show on minimalism, I think your place could qualify. But I may still trade with you." He smiled and led the way to the car. "You smell nice and look lovely." What could she say but, "Thank you." She wished she was wearing all her hospital garments and had skipped the perfume. She had always hated attention.

"Did you ever watch the John Wayne movie *The Quiet Man?* He asked.

"Yes, with that actress, Maureen O'Hara? People used to say I looked like her, before we had to hide our faces. I probably have her personality too."

When they walked into "Mandalay" as she called it, but only in her mind, the doctor motioned for her to leave her watch on the entryway table. They both removed them, then he put his finger to his lips. They went to the kitchen.

"I have received word that more people are being monitored through their phones. The practice stopped for a while, but we cannot say anything while those watches are on or near us. Not that we would say anything rebellious or that would make us appear to be insurrectionists. But we cannot be too careful. They chatted about hospital policies and the overreach in the laboratory and what could be changed. "Hospital administrators only have so much authority," then Chris added, "hamburgers are ready."

"Don't forget, you promised to show me your food larder."

"As long as you play another tune on the piano."

After he showed her his food and freezer bunker, she tried to remember more of her memorized piano tunes. They sat across from each other in the den, and he became serious again. "A friend gave me a newspaper that has spelled out some pretty draconian ideas coming out of Pharm-6, plus information on crises in other parts of the world. I am concerned that we aren't going to have a say as doctors on what we believe is correct treatment protocol, and I think the Privacy Act is going to be defunct. There won't be any more right to privacy." He let that soak in. "I am seriously thinking of going on strike, and more doctors are agreeing."

"How do you know this?"

"There is an underground network using ham radios, and that newspaper that I think is run by a kid in a basement, is becoming very effective. We have been kept in the dark for a very long time. I can't in good conscience continue to go along with it."

"Can you afford not to work? Is that why you want to trade places?" She smiled knowing it wasn't.

"I am worried about your job being in jeopardy. If they find out that we are friends and are hanging out together, there could be serious ramifications. I think from now on our watches stay home when we are together," he wasn't smiling.

"Are you thinking of doing this right away?"

"I thought of what you said, and I am not okay with doing facelifts after only two weeks of training. It is absurd, I am a heart surgeon. Those classes start next week, and I think that is when I will resign. Lily, I've become fond of you which makes this even more difficult. But no, I don't really need to work, and I have enough food as you can see. I think long term I may need to find another job, maybe a veterinarian." He smiled. "I'm turning fifty soon, too early to retire; something will turn up. I can always sell the place and move to Texas to be closer to the kids."

Suddenly Lily was struck. To find a friend then lose him in a week, it was too much to think about. "I think I am ready to protest also. I already told you that I will not do facelifts. Are they really going to mandate this?"

"Our informant says yes, and we will probably get that notice this week."

"I am going to quit too then. I guess I will have to move out of my apartment. They give us two weeks to evacuate. I'll find something else," she was mostly talking to herself.

"Do you have any savings?" His mind was now finding solutions.

"I haven't spent a dime in 15 years, so yes, I will be fine."

"Marry me, Lily. I think we could make a great team, maybe even open a clinic and serve the people who would never enter a hospital."

She ignored the marriage part, "Wouldn't they take our licenses away?"

"That won't keep us from serving. Mostly what we do is prescribe drugs, set bones and maybe do a few heart surgeries, I haven't felt very needed in a long time." He knelt down, "Would you consider being my wife? Not because you feel sorry for me, but because we could be a team, and I know our love would grow. I already hate being away from you. I am always trying to make excuses to come see you. I won't beg, and I know this seems absurd, but my life is changing quickly, and I don't want to do this without you."

She couldn't talk for a few seconds, but in those seconds the war was raging. She knew that if she had been 20 years younger, she would have said yes immediately, but age brings caution, fear, and even a distaste for change. But she knew she liked him. He was the only spark she'd had in her life for a very long time. Why not, what could she lose. "Yes, I will marry you."

Chapter 9

Monday morning was electric, starting with the bus ride.

"Good morning, Dr. Lil!" Rosa was always cheerful in the morning.

"Call me Lily girls. I am getting married. Don't tell anyone yet. Okay?" whispered Dr. Lily.

They both muttered, "Sure."

Grace spoke up, "Why 'Lily' instead of 'Dr. Lil'? And are you marrying Dr. Chris?"

"That was fast." Rosa chimed in.

"'Lily' because I like it, and you two are going to be my maids of honor. And yes, it is Dr. Chris. I like his house." Then she laughed; they all laughed.

The next electric moment was when the faxes that came in requiring all doctors to take the two-week course and the on-site face lifting training with Pharmakon 6. Then came the notification that all full-time nurses had to take the esthetician course. Tables would be set up for nurses to sign up and classes would begin in two weeks. Rosa and Grace were looking forward to the training. Lily just shook her head.

Grace was also delighted when she called Cindy and asked questions about her health and new family. "I am so happy; I've gained ten pounds and look normal again. Mom and Dad are great, and they are trying to adopt me, can you believe it! You are the best nurse in the world, and I am going to be a nurse when I grow up!" Cindy chattered on, and when they hung up Grace felt like all that she had gone through in the last ten years, at that moment, made it worth it. Nothing could possibly dampen her spirits.

The three friends met for lunch. "Girls, I have to tell you that Dr. Chris and I are quitting our jobs. We cannot agree to do facelifts, nor do we feel like two weeks training is enough. We will give our notice on Thursday, but the hospital will be required to let us go immediately because we won't sign the agreement. We are also going to take out our savings from our hospital pensions. Taxes will be high but crossing the powers that be may provoke them to punish us by emptying our accounts. Chris has a safe, and if you two ever need anything just let me know. We will keep in touch, I promise. This means I have less than three weeks to plan a wedding, so if you have any ideas let me know." They chatted about venues and decided that the crowd would be small, so the doctor's fancy house would do just fine. She would have to find a dress. Rosa said she would find a bakery that would do the cake, and Grace said she would take care of the flowers. They had a quick conversation again on the bus ride home, Dr. Lily had only three minutes to talk before her stop.

"Can you believe this?" Rosa shook her head. "I had a feeling, but that was fast!"

"I guess we have a wedding to plan which is good. It will keep us from getting sad about her leaving us." She lowered her voice to a whisper. "Do you think Pharm-6 is a corrupt company?" Her spirits had become dampened.

Grace walked to the park, but Jonathan wasn't there. She knew he was working on his next paper and using her ledger to do so. She didn't see him for a week.

"Grace, please talk to Stephen, make sure he remembers about tonight's dinner at Mary's house. I suppose we may not be wearing our PPE garb, but we can wear it over there just in case. Make sure he knows this. I am assuming he has nothing to hide because he was born in Canada." Dr. Lily prepared them for the evening on the bus ride to work. "I will pick you up with the hospital car at 5:30. Tell Stephen that too." Grace nodded. "Rosa, how is the cake coming? I can't believe I'm getting married in four days. We have a final count of 25 people."

"The cake will be perfect. Did you find some way to get coffee?" Rosa asked. Grace noticed her boss's animated behavior.

"You are right, I am rather wired, but it is probably adrenalin, but maybe coffee-the groom has plenty. I am getting married, quitting my job and moving. A lot of stress markers right now. I just have to get through it."

Grace took the elevator to the basement and knocked on the glassed-in office of the head of laboratory operations, Stephen Holt.

"Hi, come in."

"I'm here to relay a message from Dr. Lil. She said she will pick us up around 5:30, and we are going to wear our personal protective garments, but we may be asked to remove them so wear something underneath." She smiled, but of course, he couldn't see it.

"I'm not very good at being sociable. I work long hours, and on my days off I play video games. I think it would be a mistake. Can you make excuses for me?"

"I think this is part of the agreement that allowed you to keep your job, Stephen, don't make me make my boss angry! You won't have to talk; just eat and smile occasionally. Two hours max, then we go home. Okay?"

"Does the doctor have my address?"

"Yes, she does, see you tonight."

There was no mistaking that Stephen was a brilliant scientist but low on social skills, but she, in fact, was feeling nervous also. *What is wrong with us that we don't want to get together and have a bit of friendly conversation?* She rode the elevator to her floor and spent the day admitting a few emergency room patients.

The ride to the dinner party was quiet after they picked Stephen up at his apartment building two miles from the hospital. They couldn't really talk about the wedding with a man in the car. Grace mentioned some of the patients that had come in that day, a boy with a stye, a man with heart pain, two women needing the med bed for the relief of pain and infection that had invaded open sores. The med bed procedure was expensive, so it wasn't often used, but it was sure a successful way to bring some relief. Rosa agreed, and commented that she wished it was less expensive, and that insurance companies would cover it. Lily remarked that insurance companies covered little these days, so the medical field had been forced to drop prices. This made little difference on whether people could afford treatments or not. Stephen remained silent.

The group knocked on the door of a rather large home, Grace hoped that Mary hadn't forgotten about the dinner plans; Stephen hoped she had. The door swung open, and a ten-year-old girl welcomed them. "Please come in, we are so happy that you could come. I am Grace; Mom is finishing up in the kitchen. "Why don't you come meet my family?" She led them to a large sitting room next to the front door and another three children greeted them. "Take off those hats so we can see your faces and hair. Come sit by me! I'm Celeste and this is Joseph. Baby Mercy is sleeping, but you can see her when she wakes up." Just then a man walked in and interrupted the scene.

"I am Todd, Mary's husband, please take your robes off; you can hang them on this coat rack. It looks like you have met the children. This is Celeste, Joseph, Grace, Timothy and Mercy is asleep." They shook hands, and introductions were made.

"My name is Grace also!" commented Grace to the 10-year-old. It was nice that the two had an instant connection. They sat at a large table; the children had already eaten, so they were dismissed to go and play. The conversation started off slowly, but soon it was relaxed, and even Stephen seemed to enjoy himself. He was mostly excited about the food.

61

"This is so good. I haven't had a home cooked meal in years! Thank you for having us over." That was the extent of his voluntary input for the evening except for when Mary brought out chocolate cake and served coffee. "Wow, coffee and cake. I love it. Have you tried that chicory drink at the cafeteria? Dreadful stuff."

They talked about the new rules, but Lily steered away from the conversation. Then when Mary had them move into the school room, Lily signaled to them to remove their hospital watches. The four of them left the devices on the table.

"What is that about?" Stephen whispered to Grace.

"I don't know, I think she will let us know."

They entered a decorated school room with bookcases full of children's schoolbooks, tables, small chairs, and a whiteboard.

"I homeschool the children. We don't watch the television school. I don't think the government thought about large families not having enough televisions for this public program. I prefer to have them together where they can interact and help each other." The hospital group was amazed. In an era where children were rare and unseen, this was like going back 20 years. Mary had them sit down.

"I noticed that you removed your watches. I think it is wise for you to consider that everything you say and do is being tracked. It is a good idea to be safe these days." Lilly understood, but the rest of them were confused. She continued to the front of the room, next to the large white board and a flip chart. Stephen was thinking that his punishment was now to begin.

"I want to share a few things that I have noticed in the last 10 years." She flipped to the first page of the flip chart. "This health issue is quite a mystery. Have we been so busy trying to find a cure or a solution, that we have failed to look at the bigger picture? I don't believe this is just a random problem that has appeared out of nowhere. I believe in cause and effect. Genetics can be a cause of course. Pharmakon 6 exists to research these causes, and unless they are hiding something (I think they have hidden quite a bit), they have not yet found the initial cause. So here are my questions. We will go through them one by one to see if there are any insights.

"Number one: What is the historical data on boils and the speeding of the aging of skin and eyes?"

"I only know of three places that boils occur, in the Old Testament, and one in the New Testament of the Bible," replied Rosa.

"I have only heard of boils in tropical areas of the world caused by the staphylococcus bacteria. Only aging and rare skin disorders cause the other symptoms." Lily added.

"Number two: What has history told us about these causes?"

"It is usually an infection caused by staph. But antibiotics aren't working." Lily again answered.

"Three: Is an undiscovered staph infection the cause; or one that we can't see under a microscope?"

"Stephen, what do you say?" They looked at the expert who stumbled over his words. "You are right, we can't seem to see much under the microscopes. The electron microscope would be better for this, but at 10 million dollars, I won't be getting one any time soon. Reports and conclusions have come out, but to be honest, I would like to repeat those experiments, because I am not trusting the procedures or the methods."

"Four: Can something be smaller than a virus, or is this a smaller virus or maybe part of one?" Again, they looked at Stephen to answer.

"I suppose so."

"Five: Where exactly are these sores located? Notice that only a few nurses can collect this data, and they are not allowed to pass it on unless hired by the Pharm group."

"Grace and I have noticed that they are located mostly on the face and neck and seem to follow nerve endings which is what makes them more painful than normal. But we have seen them on all parts of the body. I have heard from a few elderly patients who told me the pain is similar to shingles." Rosa remarked.

"Six: Can we deduce anything from where most of these boils occur?" They shook their heads no. Rosa spoke up again, "These are not the usual blisters of shingles nor are they the staph-caused boils we have seen in the past. We are dealing with a new mystery disease not seen before the last 13 years." The group let that sink in before Mary began again.

"Seven: Who are being affected? Do we even know that other countries are not unaffected?"

This is something Grace had carefully noted in her ledger. "I have seen it rarely in children younger than 6 or 7. Teenagers don't like to come to the ER because of the mess this infection has made of their faces, but from what I have seen, nearly all ages are affected, but not as many of the elderly. But let us be clear about the fact that it is against the law to ask anything about their infection status unless they do come into the hospital, and we cannot see people unless they give us permission. We have no idea what we are dealing with now after 10 years of research which has been stifled by rules. No one from other countries working at the hospital are infected. In fact, we haven't lost any doctors or nurses from infection in a long time."

"Eight: Who do you know personally that are affected?" Mary asked. There was a long pause.

"Only the ones that have come into the ER." They nodded, and Grace continued. "My brother is infected, I think. I haven't seen him in 10 years. I just saw the worst case in the ER a few weeks ago. She is 13 years old, and it was gruesome." Grace inputted.

"What was her state of mind? Mary probed.

"Well, I didn't want to say it, but she had just killed her grandmother. They deemed it self-defense, but she was still awfully emotional about it."

"Lastly, the biggest and most important question; is it truly an infectious disease?" Mary continued, "We don't know. I think that our country is at a stand-still. And because the focus has been on our outerwear, the laws and containment practices, we may never get to the bottom of this as a nation. I do think though, that there are people out there that have solved the problem, but they do not have a voice, or they know they won't be listened to. Simple solutions, if discovered, will make this country a laughingstock of the world. We are floundering and in the dark. Our homeschool is studying the writings of JRR

Tolkien, and in the *Hobbit* it is said, 'Where sickness thrives, bad things will follow.' That is what we are seeing now." Mary ended her speech.

Dr. Lily asked one question of her own directed at Mary. "Do you know if it is infectious?"

"I only have a hypothesis." She then changed the subject. "Stephen, I am so glad you came tonight, and I want to extend an invitation to you to come any Tuesday that you are free. I will set a place for you. I would love to hear more about what you have discovered. Would you be open to that?"

"Thank you, yes, I will bring my notes. I will be here unless I call. I can get your number from the office."

Mary continued to the group, "Don't forget your watches, and don't forget to remove them when you discuss these and similar matters. I have heard a rumor that so called Chinese peace-keeping forces are on their way to enforce the rules in communities that are not in compliance with the regulations." Dr. Lily hung back as the group walked out the door.

"I have heard those rumors also. Dr. Chris and I are quitting our jobs; we are being forced to do facelifts with only 2 weeks of training. Also, we getting married on Sunday; 3:00, at Doctor Chris's house, and we would love it if your whole family could attend. Here is the address." She whispered and handed Mary a slip of paper. "Dinner was fabulous, and your family is delightful."

Chapter 10

The wedding was beautiful. Lily bought the perfect dress at a thrift shop but never told anyone where she found it. The lace-covered, pure white, mid-calf length dress looked expensive. Her curled auburn hair was pinned back, and she carried a bouquet of red roses that Grace provided. The cake was enormous, much bigger than 30 guests could eat. It even had a little figurine of a bride and groom on top. Mary and Todd's five children came which livened up the party. They took turns reciting memorized poetry and passages from famous works. Lily played the piano for the group and 10-year-old Grace played her recital pieces. Troubles were forgotten and laughter was healing souls. Stephen came for the cake and coffee but found himself joining in and having fun.

"Grace, can you take my work car and give Rosa a ride home then return it in in the morning? Chris has a pick-up truck, so we will head to work early in the morning and empty our offices." Grace frowned to show she was sad then took the keys.

"We are going to miss you so much!" They hugged and the house emptied quickly.

Grace dropped off Rosa then turned left and drove to the rabbi's home. "Come in." the rabbi was on his easy chair. "Oh, it's you, I was hoping you would come. My arm is itching so badly, I want this thing off!"

"Do you have a hanger?"

"Yes, in the bedroom." Grace untwisted a hanger and showed him how to carefully insert it under the cast to relieve the itch. "I have a doctor friend who will take this off. He said that we need to give it three more weeks."

"Jonathan is in the garage. The rebels are deep in slaughter. I will discipline all of them." He turned his head and closed his eyes. For a few minutes she studied his wrinkled face, long gray hair and beard and his long thin nose. She was growing fond of the elderly man and wondered about his past.

She slowly opened the side door of the old two-car garage. It was full of light and noise. Jonathan was printing his newspapers and was deep in thought. She stood there and wondered how to get his attention. She waited until the machine stopped running then she turned the lights off and on again. He spun around and saw her waving. He walked over, gave her a quick hug. "What are you doing here? You look great!"

"I just came from my friend's wedding, Dr. Lily married Dr. Chris. She gave me the company car so I could drive my friend home."

"I didn't know you drove."

"It has been a while, but it came back to me. I thought I'd check up on my patient."

"And friend?" He asked.

"Yes, I am missing my ledger which has been my friend for thirteen years." She smiled.

"It's right here, I was going to return it tomorrow. Your book has kept me busy, and this is going to be the best and longest edition. I should be finished by midnight so I can bring you a copy tomorrow."

"How do you distribute them?"

"I open the garage and people come and take as many as they want, then go and hand them out very carefully and secretively. Most come after dark, some bring wheelbarrows, baby carriages, back packs, and even a milk man pretending to deliver milk shows up early in the morning and carts off a bunch. I have people that come who have regular border passes for one reason or another and can cross state lines. They go from North Carolina to the surrounding states, even all the way up to Washington DC. I am expecting to have to do a second printing. This one will be popular. It's all thanks to you."

Grace picked up the book, "I took a hanger and unbent it so the rabbi could itch his arm. He has three more weeks before the cast can be removed. He said something odd. I am going to start writing down his words in here." She tapped her book; they said their goodbyes, and she drove home with a full heart. A nagging thought disrupted her happiness, *maybe this thing is not infectious. I need to know. How can I figure this out?* Her night was not one with sleep, partly from the coffee at the wedding, and partly because she felt a responsibility to find a cause and a cure. She tossed and turned. Before the dim autumn sun rose, she had decided, and it was a very serious decision.

Monday never felt more like a Monday. The two doctors were gone before Grace and Rosa had arrived. There was a table set up in the hallway just past the metal detector where every doctor and nurse had to sign up for new skin treatment and surgery training. The table would only be there for three days. There was a sign up for the first shift, and one for the second. Grace did not want to go to a class after work, so she and Rosa signed up for the one at noon. "We just need to get a few nurses to work for us for two hours. I'm sure we can manage." Grace didn't want to miss her walks to the park. As they passed the admin office the pair refused to look through the glass. It was too sad. "We have a week before this training begins." Rosa whispered. "Try to have a good day."

Grace wanted to tell Rosa her plan but knew that she would try to talk her out of it. She had made her choice, and no one was going to dissuade her, not even Jonathan. She bundled up and trotted to the park. Jonathan was already there holding a newspaper. "Hi, do you want to come over? It is cold out here."

"Sure." Jonathan trotted to keep up with her.

"What's the hurry?"

"I have something to tell you, and I am not asking for your advice; I am just going to tell you because I need someone to support my decision and help me if I encounter problems."

After sitting down, Grace continued, "This is what I wrestled with all night long, and I have to do this. We went to the house of one of our nurses; I think she may read your paper. Anyway, she said she had 25 questions to ask. We went through 9 of them, and the last one bothered me. It was whether this

70

disease was infectious. Think about this, Jonathan, it is the main question. It has shut down our country. I am going to experiment on myself to find out." She paused to read his expression. He leaned back into the couch.

"I would hate to lose you just when I found you, but I know that this has been your passion for a long time, and I understand passion. I will support you and stick by you if this experiment has negative results. What is your plan?"

"I want to find someone who is really sick. I want to drink after them, shake their hand and," she paused, "I am going to insert contents of a boil into a self-inflicted wound, not once but twice." Jonathan was quiet for a moment. "What if the disease is only in the blood?"

"Then we will know at the very least that it is only transferred by blood and not by anything else." She hadn't thought of that but wasn't going to start experimenting with blood just yet.

"I will find someone for you. When do you want to do this?"

"Right now," she answered. In the kitchen she found a cheese grater, disinfected it and her forearm, then she scraped the skin until it drew blood. She checked the supplies in her work bag, then nodded to Jonathan.

"Okay, let's go. It is a long walk, but I can drive you home." She had a better idea. After a call to Dr. Lily who, as her last act as the hospital employee, was able to get the authorization for the bus to give them a ride to check up on the rabbi. Grace gowned up and gave Jonathan her extra robe.

"Are you kidding me?"

"We need to look like the professionals that we are," she insisted.

"Won't they notice the name?" She placed a piece of duct tape over her name.

The bus driver dropped them off then the pair looked in on the sleeping rabbi. "Does he have a name?" she whispered.

Jonathan chuckled, "Jonathan, that is why we call him the rabbi. Let's go for a walk." They walked for more than six blocks when the neighborhood suddenly changed. Poverty and a stench filled the atmosphere. He walked up to a house and knocked.

"Come in," a faint replay was heard.

"We are going door to door to see if anyone here needs to see a nurse," Grace loudly proclaimed. In the shadows they saw a hooded figure.

"Yeah, I could use a nurse." The smell was horrid, a little like skunk and sewer back-up. Using her little flashlight, she looked into his eyes and saw the ectropion signs of the sagging lower eye lid. She saw drugs on the table.

"What are you taking for the pain?"

"Mostly dope, it doesn't work though, just keeps me tired. Friends bring me whatever comes their way, but they hurt too, so I don't see them much."

"How are you getting food?" Grace was feeling panicky.

"There are nice people in the neighborhood that bring me our rations. I have three roommates who are in the back sleeping. We do okay."

"Where do you hurt mostly?"

"I would rather not say."

"I brought four bottles of pain killer, one for each of you in the house. Please only take one in the morning and one at night. Usually, people take one a day, but I will come back in two weeks and bring more and see how you are doing."

"That's nice. Thanks." He shivered and sat down.

Grace opened her bag and pulled out a sealed cup of water that they use for hospital patients. "Drink this first, it is just to make sure you are hydrated," she lied. She put the cup in a sterile bag then pulled up his sleeve and tried not to gag. "I am going to disinfect this area and take a sample so we can see if there is anything else we can give you." It was another lie, but she wanted to give him a little hope.

She gently rubbed an alcohol pad on the largest boil on his arm. He groaned in pain.

"I could lance this if you want but first let me try to drain it. She poked the needle straight into the boil to avoid hitting a nerve and pulled the plunger. Very little came out. "It is too thick. I can quickly lance it, and bandage it if you want?"

"Go ahead, but this isn't the one that hurts the most."

"I wish I could get you into a med bed, it would be so comforting and cleansing. Would you be open to a trip to the hospital?"

"I'll think about it." She lanced and wiped the offensive sore and asked Jonathan to bandage it. He did, and she turned around and wiped the mess onto her scraped arm. She promised the patient that she would be back then fled the house.

"I changed my mind. I am only doing that once." She took out the cup and licked the outside rim.

"Don't you worry about getting other diseases?"

"No. Just look at what they are going through!" Her heart was breaking.

"Grace, have you wondered why the stats on crime has dropped? This is the neighborhood that came and pillaged the rabbi's house eight years ago."

"We need to help them. The hospital, backed by the government, gives certain people free care. I am pretty sure that this guy qualifies."

"Let's get you home before curfew. If you aren't at the park tomorrow, I will be at your house."

"Stalker!" They laughed. She was too tired to read his newspaper

Chapter 11

The election was largely ignored. People watched the candidates talk every night on the news for a month. Debating took too much energy and people in pain aren't successful at defending their views. At first, millions tuned in each week, until at the end, only a few thousand. Everyone had already decided who they wanted as a figurehead leader of the country. Each of the two men running for the office of president talked for two minutes, then each running mate was given the same amount of time. On November 11th, every American was able to log on to their computer and with fingerprint and eye scanner, vote.

Joshua Conner had a handsome face before the plague attacked it. The CGI talents of the weekly news editors were able to bring back youth and banish most blemishes on Mr. Conner, but his running mate, Mae Bronson, needed no cover-up, and no make-up. She was a beautiful woman in her 60's whom Conner had chosen because of her success as governor of West Virginia. She had kept her state from falling into the poverty and disrepair that most states had succumbed to during the crisis. She was bold and direct and had more energy than the other three who appeared weekly on camera. The people liked her. Jorge, Mr. Conner's campaign manager was the one who presented her name to him, and her wise orations seemed to be paying off.

The other candidate, Ben Fleming, had been President James's vice president and then became president for two years when President James suddenly passed away in 2038. He was soft spoken but had a lot to say about the economy and how he had hoped to bring down the cost of living.

President Ben Flemming had to be coerced to run for the office of president by several in congress and finally by Dr. Orillion himself. It only took one phone call. The doctor also gave him a name of someone he could choose as a running mate. The doctor's plan backfired as the former president began presenting innovative ideas making the leader of Pharm-6 nervous, who soon switched sides and began to covertly project an image of the former president as weak and impotent, and Mr. Conner as strong with leadership skills. The nightly news editors made this possible. The opposite was actually true, but it had worked. President Conner won by a slim margin and a celebration was held in the ballroom of New York City's Luxury Suites with 100 in attendance. Short speeches were given, and the new president made sure to give much credit to his campaign manager and his new vice president, Mae Bronson.

Madam Bronson drove home soberly that night knowing that if she played her cards right, she would be able to slowly turn the political ship around. Her husband had passed away from a heart attack ten years ago. She had married him when she was forty, he was 60. They were both involved in helping shape government policies from their Washington DC offices. She was a senator; he was a lawyer. Now her focus was on how to proceed with her plans to improve the nation while being roped to a man she knew was too sick to have a backbone. It was difficult finding anyone who was willing to serve.

Out of nowhere came a semi-truck driving in the lane of the newly elected vice president, and in seconds her Mercedes Benz was in the ditch, she was unconscious, and the semi exploded. The crash was so odd that investigators spent months trying to figure out how it had happened, who had been in the semi, and how she had survived but remained in a coma.

The president of the United State, President Conner, the youngest since JFK, moaned from the pain. He was sick and tired of the stupid pharmacy group not coming up with a solution. "They are stealing our money," he said aloud. He laid back on his couch and tried to get comfortable. "I'd fire them all if I could," again grumbling to an empty room. He popped another pain pill. A knock on the door made him slowly sit up.

"Yes? Come in." He quickly put on his face covering, purple to match his robe.

A small man draped in green, the color of the white house aides and government workers, entered. It was the new president's very faithful campaign manager and aide, Jorge, who was the only one allowed to disturb the president.

"You have an urgent call; it is the president of Pharmakon 6."

"Bring me the phone. Hello, Dr. Orillion, I was just thinking about you." He tried not to sound irritated.

"Thank you, I have a new and tested drug, and it works wonders for pain and swelling. I can have it sent over if you would like?" Dr. Orillion's voice had a soothing quality to it.

"Yes, please!" He couldn't hide the excitement he felt. A small package arrived for him, and his aide opened it up and read the label.

"Only one a day for a week, then you can take two." Jorge handed him a pill and water. He then put the bottle on a bookshelf on the other side of the room. He did not want the president to overdose. Jorge Silva was a descendant of Portuguese great grandparents who immigrated to Hawaii during the sugarcane boon, then his grandparents moved to New York in the 60's. They worked hard to give their children and grandchildren the best education and would have been proud of how Jorge was serving the country by serving the president. He had the heart of a servant and was also a fabulous speech writer. He worked tirelessly on the president's campaign and was probably the main reason the president won the election two years ago.

"Mr. President!" Jorge had been knocking with no answer. He cracked open the door and sprawled across the couch was the president snoring. Jorge shook him, yelled at him, even pinched him to no avail. The White House doctor was called, and the president was rushed to the hospital. "What has he taken?" The doctor asked Jorge, then Pharm-6 was called.

"Had he taken any other drugs along with the new one?" was their response. No one knew. The president was hooked up to IVs and for fourteen hours the president slept like a baby. He would have been happy for the rest if he hadn't woken up in the hospital. He was furious and would have had more of a tantrum, but he hurt too much.

"Where is my mask!" He demanded. He did not want anyone to see his 45-year-old face that looked more like a 65-year-old face. Pharm-6 had just experienced its first major failure, and it was a big one. The pain killer that the president took along with the new drug caused the reaction, but there had been no warning on the label.

Janitor Joe had worked for twenty years cleaning the building that now housed Pharmakon 6. He always wore sound muffling headphones while pushing his cart from room to room. He picked his own hours, clocked in and out, and was so unassuming that no one paid attention to him. His large yellow cart held the vacuum and the cleaning supplies needed for the job. He chose to work on floor 23 during the time the Pharm team had their morning 10:00 meeting. Joe would let his headphones slip; he would wash windows, dust around the secretary's room, and he heard every word behind the closed door. He emptied the trash receptacles and always kept every scrap of paper. With gloved hands he would place them in a bag that later was hidden in his extra-large, black tin lunch pail. Every Tuesday night, a small gathering came to Joe and Georgia's house for the sorting of the papers. Everyone wore gloves and Georgia took notes. The meeting usually lasted two hours, and after the last scrap was studied and encoded, notes were taken, then the originals were incinerated in the back yard. Many secrets were revealed from those pieces of paper. Joe, from memory, would report on what had been spoken in the meetings and overheard from Dr. Orillion's phone conversations. Then notes were given to those with CB radios who then sent Herb, one of the ham radio operators, the encoded messages. He had a long-range ham radio relaying the news to Jonathan. Before dawn, the messages would be sent out, and Joe was back at work.

It had been a week since the last newspaper had been passed around, so it was time for the next one to reach Washington DC. No meeting was scheduled that morning among the pharmacy group. Joe cleaned the cafeteria and thought about going home early until he saw several of the 6 walking quickly toward the conference room. Joe pushed his cart into the elevator and arrived on the 23rd floor in time to see the conference door close. What he heard was startling and confirmed everything he believed about the group.

Dr Orillion's voice was loud, "This was turned in by one of our lab techs. Apparently, his mother received a copy. It has very disturbing and maligning information about our company and our work. Word has leaked out about the president's stay in the hospital. Our reputation is at stake. We may have another mole in the company. How did they know about the president? Was someone at the hospital a traitor? We must find the sources and crush them! Lu, I want the tech and his mother to disappear."

"Do you mean fired?"

"No! you know what I mean. They cannot spread this propaganda any further. It is time to use half of our police force to track people and listen to their conversations using phone and television spying equipment. Lu, I want you to head this up quickly. They can begin to go through old data that we have stored. Now is the time to comb through it and eliminate the insurrectionists! Any questions?" That is when the group usually stood up to leave. Joe grabbed his cart a flew to the other side of the room. He fished out of the bottom of his cart a cold cup of coffee that he had saved for such emergencies He poured it on the carpet then fell down and begin scrubbing it while slipping on his headphones and pretending not to hear anything happening behind him. No one except Jacques noticed the bent over elderly spy. "What are you doing here?" He asked loudly then harshly kicked the janitor's shoe after noticing the headphones. Jacques knew that the janitor wasn't usually cleaning the offices at that time of day.

"Someone spilled the coffee on the carpet, I could not just leave it until the morning. I didn't want the stain to set and leave a permanent mark." Joe managed to keep cool, and the man seemed to believe the lie. If he had asked around, he would have known it was a lie.

Joe was still shaking when he arrived home. "Invite the group over for pie, tell them to leave electronics at home." "Pie" was the secret emergency code for the group. They arrived within fifteen minutes and quickly saw that Joe was having a hard time speaking.

"Any telephones?" Joe asked.

"No," the group became frightened.

Joe turned on the television then shut the kitchen door where they sat at the extra-long table. Joe and Georgia had raised six children in that house and now were raising an army.

"Someone at the company turned in one of our papers to Orillion. His mother was receiving them. They are both going to be murdered. Probably tonight and there is not a thing I can do about it, because I don't know who he is!"

"Who is going to murder them?"

"Pharm-6." The room grew quiet. It was hard to believe.

"Are you sure you heard correctly?"

"Loud and clear! Not only that, but they are going to go through old phone recordings to try and find links to our group. They can even watch us through our TVs. This is terrifying! We have to alert the entire group tonight but be careful. Hide all your phones. Don't turn them off just make sure they cannot hear you." He buried his head in his hands for a moment. "Didn't we know this day was coming? Didn't we make a pact to never give in to fear?" They nodded in agreement. "So, let's get to it, and close in prayer."

Chapter 12

Grace finally took time to sit and read Jonathan's article from her ledger. She scanned it first then read every detail. It was like reviewing her own history. Grace had forgotten about the 400 FEMA camps that the first 200,000 people were taken to so the "plague" wouldn't spread. They were outcasts, the pariah of society who wouldn't comply with the new rules of "isolation to destroy infection." Jonathan added that when the politicians, lawyers and judges started showing signs of the infirmity, they opened the gates to the camps. Maybe the pain made walking a torture so they couldn't leave. Maybe those people are still there, being fed and taken care of by our government. Are pain killers still being provided? He wrote that there was little information concerning this neglected group of people.

Jonathan had the article so well organized, something she hadn't thought of doing. After writing about the first year of Americans being sent home and non-Americans leaving the country, and only U.S. government planes flying internationally, he listed the second-year progress (or non-progress). He wrote that no one knew by the end of the second year who were sick; people were beginning to be hidden behind masks. All schooling was done at home and so were nearly all businesses. The disenfranchised pharmaceutical company's ugly past was reported for anyone who had forgotten about the test group who had volunteered to be experimented on and who had died as a result. This gave Grace a moment of pain.

That is when the food trains began rolling across the country. Only those who had stored up food and supplies were prepared, the rest had to eat the mystery fare shipped in from China. Grace remembered seeing 'Made in China' on the bottom of the trays. Grace was glad he added that point. PPI, protected personal information laws were fully implemented and had terrible consequences. Only in hospitals could people be asked personal questions and even then, certain questions could not be asked. Even search engines were shut down.

By the third-year, people refused to enter hospitals and clinics. They came to believe that the infection was being spread in these venues which made research difficult. Church gatherings, and any gathering larger than the number of people in one's family was banned. Thousands of doctors, nurses, teachers and professors were hired from Mexico, South America, the Philippines and India. These were quickly trained and sent to hospitals, schools and universities around the country. He added all the governmental laws and mandates that flooded the country in the fourth year.

Then the people had voted in the first gay president whose infirm partner had to live at home with his mother. He reported that the country's debt was now 60 trillion dollars. Borrowing foreign workers was not a cheap endeavor.

He then reviewed Pharmakon 6's history. The media, entertainment, and television stations were completely controlled and became purely educational. It was clear that Pharmakon 6 was in control and the government was just a front. That is when social media was banned. He revealed that the reason given by Pharm-6 was the selfies showing the brutal results of the disease were scaring the psyche of children. Jonathan surmised that part of this move was because the resulting anger of seeing these images began unifying the people. Phones could be used only for phone calls. Jonathan reported something Grace did not know; several million cell phones went dark. The reason given was that people could no longer afford them.

Jonathan then outlined what was happening in the present. People were not volunteering to be test guinea pigs. Some were secretly gathering at night to worship and discuss the emergency situations. The Chinese police force was covered. In his last line he quoted from the *Hobbit*, "The reign of the beast will end!" Grace paused. She began to worry about Jonathan. If the powers that be ever figured out who he was, that would be that end of her new friend.

She had been reading for an hour when there was a knock at the door. She opened it without even looking. Jonathan smiled and saw the paper in her hand. "Well, what do you think?"

"Brilliant, and dangerous!"

"How are you feeling?"

"Fine? Oh right." She looked at her arm. "So far so good. Do you think I could have done something more to make sure the experiment worked?"

"No! And you call me dangerous. Let's go to the kitchen and sit at the table."

"Want some tea?" He declined which made her curious.

"How is distribution going?"

"Done, and I'm starting a new batch tomorrow. This network is amazing. I have the CBers who do not transmit very far, but they connect to the Ham radios which reach longer distances. It is an amazing underground network. Where is your watch phone?"

"In the bedroom."

"I am not ignorant enough to believe that this smooth operation can go on forever. Remember Corrie ten Boom?" Jonathan's face grew grim. Grace shook her head.

"She was involved in a similar system during World War 2. Only then, the underground workers used bicycles, and they were passing around babies and hiding people to keep them safe. I am not afraid of getting arrested; I am afraid that our progress will wane if I do."

"I could not bear to lose you now. How can I help?"

"Keep your eyes and ears open and keep me posted. I have to tell you something, where's your phone?"

"In the bedroom, you already asked me that. What's going on?"

"They found my last paper, and they are going to kill the lab tech who turned it in and his mother who was the owner. It is getting very serious. They are starting to go through old recordings from phones and televisions. We cannot be too careful. I think I should not visit for a while. I don't want them to connect you and your network of friends with me and my papers. I did not realize how evil this pharmacy company is, but I am sure of the intel that I received."

"Who is on the inside that is able to get this information out?"

"I will tell you someday, there are many things I would like to tell you, and I promise that I will sometime in the future. It is better to be innocent right now, and truthfully be able to say that you have no knowledge of where it comes from. You must know that a relationship with me is dangerous, so we must keep from being involved with each other." He picked up her arm and looked for boils.

"It's too late, I am involved, but I understand. This will all end soon." She switched to her stoic side and changed the subject.

"Did I tell you that all doctors must be trained in facial surgeries, or they will get fired, and all nurses are required to become estheticians? I have training starting Monday for two hours a day for two weeks. I think I told you that is why the hospital administrative doctors quit their jobs."

"I will add that to my next paper. Keep writing things down. You may need to find a really good hiding place for your journals in case you are raided by the police."

"Really? Okay, you are right though. They will slowly move closer and closer to the source of the news. Be careful."

"You also." He rose to leave and kissed her on the forehead. She wondered if it was because she might be infectious or was he just trying to stay uninvolved.

Chapter 13

Stephen again visited Mary and Todd's house. He wondered why they invited him and no one else. He felt honored, but mostly he loved the food; lasagna was his favorite, and dessert was always on the menu. He was filling out again and decided to start going to the hospital gym before work every morning. Stephen and Mary always headed off to the school room after dinner, and while Todd put the children to bed, the two scientists went to work. Stephen shared his findings and even used the white board to draw pictures. He talked about his frustrations about not having access to an electron microscope. He became so comfortable that he shared his personal struggles about feeling like he didn't fit in and about missing his family. The closed border kept him from visiting his Canadian family.

"That is rough Stephen, I think this crisis will end soon, and you will be able to go home. I want to show you something I came up with." She drew a fraction on the board. "The top number is one and represents you. You cannot be divided so I will put a zero on the bottom. Dividing by zero when graphed, moves toward infinity, but it never arrives at infinity, thus they call dividing by zero undefined because it is undefinable."

"Zero can't be a divisor," he stated but didn't like the feeling of being schooled about basics.

"Correct, now here is another fraction, the one on top represents you again and, on the bottom..." She drew the sign for infinity. "This represents what the Creator knows in His entirety. Think about this, Stephen, the more you divide yourself by infinity, the smaller you get, and the more you divide yourself by nothing, you can get close but never arrive. But if you can connect with the creator, by putting infinity at the top and you at the bottom, then you can get answers. You will be connected to truth. Our main problem during this hidden terror is that we haven't connected to the Truth."

Stephen drove home that night pondering Mary's example. It bothered him that she had crossed a line between professional and personal. He respected her ideas and found them challenging, but she seemed to be insulting him, even calling him stupid. He was raised on evolution, all scientists were, but he couldn't deny the comparison between his emptiness and discouragement and her happiness and contentment. *I probably make three times more money than she does!* He wrestled with his thoughts and finally slept dreaming of numbers, all in scientific notation.

After two weeks of training Rosa and Grace passed their esthetician tests. The government was sending the graduates creams, gels and tools that an experienced esthetician would need. "I think we won't have time to do both jobs. It takes an hour per patient for these skin procedures. Seems it is just another money maker," Rosa stated.

"Not only that, but insurance doesn't cover any of it. I agree, it makes no sense. The doctors at our hospital are scheduled for their practice face-lift surgery during the month of March. How are they going to train the whole country of doctors? It may take a year. The video classes have started, but the Pharm DC training takes a week. How do we run a hospital without the doctors?" Grace shook her head.

"How is your boyfriend?" Rosa smiled with her eyes.

"Still a boy and still just a friend. He kissed me on the forehead!"

"Wow, that's weird."

"I did an experiment, Rosa. I purposely exposed myself through the skin and through drinking after someone with a very bad case of the disease. It has been a month, and I have had no symptoms. Not even of other diseases the guy may have had. I visited him again to deliver pain killers and to offer him a ride to the hospital, but he decided not to come," whispered Grace.

"That was stupid!" Rosa was horrified.

"Shh! I know, but I had to find out if this thing is contagious. It is not!" Grace was adamant.

"One person, one experiment does not determine a result. You need to follow the scientific method." Rosa whispered loudly.

"And how do you think I should do that? Do you want to volunteer to repeat the process?" Grace had never been annoyed with Rosa before.

"No way! I have seen what it does. You were crazy to do that!"

"Well, let's agree to disagree and not bring it up again, okay?"

"I'm sorry, Grace, you did a very brave thing. I just couldn't bear seeing you get hurt." She gave her a quick hug and hopped off the bus. Grace needed cheering and was hoping Jonathan would come. The weather was too cold for a walk, but he could use the rabbi's car.

The 7:00 news came on. It was Pierre again. He encouraged everyone to stay inside and stay warm. "Snow blizzards and icy roads will be the weather for the next week or two. If you can stay inside and avoid the roads, do so. This storm is covering the entire country." It was a very low news evening.

Chapter 14

The next morning there was a note to Janitor Joe taped to his cart handle. "Clean up cubicle 32 in the lab department, toss everything." Joe made his way to the third floor and found the small area. The computer was gone. Joe dumped the rest of the items on the desk into a trash bag that was hidden inside his large trash receptacle. He wanted a chance to go through everything first before going home. He picked up the small trash can under the desk and began to dump it when he saw two pages of a newspaper, it was from The Zion Herald! Quickly hiding it deep in the inner bag, he finished his job and went to the basement to the dumpsters. No cameras were down there; it was dark and was only used for storage. He tucked the newspaper inside his pants then combed through everything else, dumping what was not important. He found a picture of a woman, probably the lab tech's mother and shoved it to the bottom of his deep trousers' pocket. He felt sick but managed to finish his day. No meetings seemed to be scheduled, and he was glad. When he arrived at home, he called another meeting. The group read every scrap of paper and took notes. They took turns looking at the picture and decided to have a solemn moment for the poor woman.

"Here is the part of the paper that he didn't turn in. Why?" He spread it out and recognized the article. "It's the one about the history of the plague the editor wrote. Maybe the lab guy read this and decided it was too inflammatory. Dr. Orillion was quick to toss everything on this boy's desk. I think they want no fingerprint proof of who sat there! I will try to find someone who can figure this out. They burned the papers and then went their separate ways; some to send messages through the airwaves."

It had been a month since Grace had seen Jonathan, and she was agitated. What if he had been arrested? She tried to distract herself with the new make-over the television stations had received. Familiar faces again reported the so-called news. Mostly they sang the praises of the Pharm corporation. Grace studied their faces and could see that they looked pretty good, just slightly altered. It was a boost to morale being able to see people again. Hairdos had changed to hide scars and lots of make-up was applied. Movies were being made and advertised on the nightly news. They were low budget with mostly talking, little action and some CGI. Again, Grace studied the faces. *I'm an esthetician now, skin is my new hobby*, she thought to herself. She loved her new focus but had yet to treat anyone. People weren't lining up to get skin treatments or facelifts in her part of the country.

She couldn't keep waiting and wondering. She bundled up and hiked the three miles to visit the rabbi. That is what she told herself. The wind was biting cold and whipped up the snow into her eyes. Her hospital garments over her winter clothes didn't seem to help much. With her bag slung over her shoulder, she finally made it. She stumbled into the house without knocking.

"Who's there?" she heard a week voice from the back bedroom. The rabbi was in bed piled with blankets.

"It's Grace, you are freezing!" The rabbi was shivering. "What can I get you?" She had an idea and ran to the kitchen. She found an old gallon water jug and filled it with hot water, wrapped it in a towel, and put it under the covers by his feet.

"That feels so good." His teeth were chattering.

"Let me see your arm." He reluctantly pulled it out from under the covers.

"See, good as new. Your friends came and removed the cast. Good people."

"Can't we turn up the heat in here?" She looked around for the thermostat.

"We can't afford it; they raised the rates so high that we only keep it on during the night."

"Where is Jonathan?" She was terrified of the answer.

"Don't worry dear, it is too cold even for the police. Very unusual for this time of year. He went to find us some food." She rubbed his hands and feet, and he finally dropped off to sleep. She washed the dishes and straightened up the house. She didn't stop moving and didn't take off her robes. Jonathan finally came in and stomped off the snow.

"Oh, looks like we have company dressed in yellow which means hospital?"

"Sorry, I couldn't stay away any longer. I had to make sure you were okay."

"I'm fine, but I don't remember March being this cold."

"Jonathan, the rabbi is too cold. He is not going to make it if we don't warm him up. I want him to come live with me. I have the extra bedroom and am able to keep the heat on all the time."

"I know! I didn't know what to do; I am so worried about him. Yes, I will take you up on your offer. We will have to get food though. Also, I have just enough gas to drive you home."

"I have a way to get food. Jonathan, please come also, I have a great couch. You can leave as soon as this cold spell is broken. I just can't stand the idea of you being here by yourself freezing to death." He nodded in submission and began to pack bags. She went in again to the rabbi.

"There is no faithfulness, no love, no acknowledgment of God in the land." The rabbi seemed out of touch with reality.

"I love you, Rabbi. You are going come and stay with me for a while." He frowned.

"I need you; I am so lonely." She thought if he considered the move as helping her, he might be more willing.

"Good idea, Grace." He seemed to snap out of his brain fog.

With great difficulty they managed to get the two settled in the small, but warm and cozy house. The rabbi was comfortable in his new surroundings. Jonathan helped him into bed piled again with blankets. Then Grace made a phone call to her old boss, Lily. She relayed the situation and within an hour a pick-up pulled up. Boxes of food were brought in, plus blankets and pillows and even a hot water bottle. The rabbi remembered the couple, "My arm is doing well, thank you." His mind again slipped into a different reality. "When they saw his sickness and sores, they turned to Assyria and sent to the great kings for help. But he is not able to cure you, not able to heal your sores. Then I will go back to my place until they admit their guilt, and they will seek my face; in their misery they will earnestly seek me." He fell asleep. Jonathan pulled out a pad of paper and wrote what had been said.

"He has been talking like this more often, and his mind isn't what it used to be," Jonathan explained to the two doctors.

"I brought a bottle of highly concentrated vitamin drops; it may help." Lily handed Grace a bottle, and they both emptied the boxes of food. Grace was so thankful especially when she saw the bag of coffee and the creamer. "This feels like Christmas!"

When everything was put away, they exchanged information. Grace started with the experiment and the adventure into the poorest part of the west side of town. Then Jonathan told the long story about his paper and how it ended up in the hands of Pharm-6, and how the section from Grace's ledger had not been included. He told about the son and his mother who were murdered. They knew the rest of the news from reading his last paper. The weather had kept him from printing for a month.

"What can we do for those drug addicts who live just six blocks from Jonathan. I'm afraid they've frozen to death!" Grace was hoping for answers.

"I went there today. I go regularly to check up on them, and they are still alive, but barely. It is so cold, and they have little body fat." Jonathan added.

Dr. Chris spoke up, "Leave it to us. Draw us a map to their house, and we will take care of them. Lily and I have been driving to different parts of town where there are needs and handing out food, clothes and drugs. I have a friend who owns a thrift shop, and he allows us to buy in bulk. I have been storing up food for years and haven't even made a dent. We will take care of them. Call us when you run out of supplies. Okay?" Jonathan and Grace nodded.

"This was quite the day." Jonathan remarked. She couldn't help it; she gave him a big hug.

They checked on the rabbi one more time. He opened his eyes and spoke, "Come, let us return. We are torn to pieces, but he will heal us; he has injured us, but he will bind up our wounds. After two days he will revive us; on the third day he will restore us. They do not cry out to me from their hearts but wail upon their beds." A tear from the corner of his closed eye slid down his face.

"He sounds like a prophet, doesn't he?"

"Yes, he does."

Chapter 15

The weather made a turn for the worse. Gales of 70 miles per hour whipped the East coast all the way through Colorado. The hospital closed down, and those employees who did not live close by had to hunker down in hospital rooms. Rosa was one of them. The cafeteria people were not there so she raided the refrigerator, grabbed two lunch plates and three puddings, then found the cook's secret stash of hot cocoa mix and his extra-large mug. She took advantage of the situation. No one else was in the room so she didn't have to feel embarrassed. She didn't even wear her head covering and mask. She was enjoying feeling full for a change when someone sat down across from her. She stopped chewing. "Hi."

"I remember you from the wedding, I'm Stephen, and you are Rosa. I see that it is a free for all in the kitchen, any culinary suggestions?"

"I left the hot cocoa out and, as you can see; I took two lunch plates. They never feed us enough. You look a little different. Did you change your hair?"

"Truthfully, I have just been putting on weight, and I started working out just to make it not pile up on my stomach."

"Okay, where are you hiding your food stash? It is time to share!" She was serious.

"Remember Mary? Of course, you do. Well, I go to her house every Tuesday for dinner; she is a great cook. I play with the children, and then she and I talk about science and the connections to this plague. I can get you invited and can pick you up. She won't care."

"I do love to eat. Make sure she really wants me, and I'm in. I can put up with a little shop talk to be able to hold that baby again."

Stephen heated up his lunch and they sat and chatted for a few hours. "Are we the only ones here?" He asked.

"The patients have been moved to the OR floor. The nurses there are on the clock during this storm. I chose not to be. They have their own lunchroom, so I guess they are probably eating better than we are."

"Let's walk around and stretch our legs. I'll take you downstairs, show you my lab and what I am working on right now."

The laboratory was impressive. Rosa had never had a reason to see it and was interested in his glassed-in office with microscopes and refrigerated blood samples.

"See this slide here? It is an experiment that I have completed now five times each with three different variables to make sure I had it right. I kept a tube of Mary's blood. Hope you didn't hear about that whole story." She nodded and patted him on the back.

"Well, I did apologize. Anyway, the variables I used was saliva, a blood sample and even a sample of the contents of a boil. When I put a sample of these on drops of Mary's blood, then on blood of someone with the plague, then comparing the tainted blood with the pure sample, Rosa, Mary's blood was not affected, but the other just looks more infected. But this is bothersome. I tested it on my blood, and my blood became tainted. Hers was unaffected. I was born in Canada so I cannot get sick, and yet my experiment says I can. Mary cannot. What do you think?"

"I am going to tell you something in confidence because I am sure she won't mind except that it was stupid. My friend did this same experiment on herself with no affect. She didn't use the ill persons blood of course, but everything else." Stephen sat down hard on his swivel chair and put his hands on his head.

"I have to tell Mary to see what she thinks. I hope the roads are clear by Tuesday."

Grace and Jonathan sat at the kitchen table. He was fidgety and getting restless and feeling useless.

"Tell me the rabbi's story." She had been curious for a while and wanted to distract him.

"He was the rabbi for a very large temple in New York. He had a wife who passed away about eleven years ago. They couldn't have children. Then he was struck, he tells me, with a passage in Isaiah and went searching for answers but wasn't satisfied with any of the other rabbis' interpretations. This passage sounds like it is about a man, but he was told that it is about the nation of Israel. His wife was the one who steered him in the right direction. She said that it sounded like the coming Messiah. He disagreed because the passage in Isaiah 53 is not a positive uplifting one. It speaks of torture and death. The Messiah was to be a victorious leader, scripture proved this to be true. Then she said something that shocked him, she wondered if this Messiah has two comings, two purposes, same man but appearing at different times in history. Grace, do you have a Bible?"

"Here it is, Isaiah 53, 'Who has believed our message?' Right there says that few will believe what is coming next. 'He grew up before him like a tender shoot.' This is talking about someone born on Earth, not an angel or even more than one man. 'He had no beauty or majesty to attract us to him.' This is not someone coming to be king. 'He was despised and rejected by men.' This stunned the rabbi. He wanted to know who could possibly be hated by his people so much that they would reject him. 'A man of sorrows, and familiar with suffering?' How could their Messiah be a man of suffering.

'Surely, he took up our infirmities and carried our sorrows. He was pierced for our transgressions, he was crushed for our iniquities; the punishment that brought us peace was upon him, and by his wounds we are healed. The Lord has laid on him the iniquity of us all. He was led like a lamb to the slaughter and as a sheep before her shearers is silent, so he did not open his mouth. He was cut off from the land of the living; for the transgression of my people, he was stricken. He was assigned a grave with the wicked, and with the rich in his death though he had done no violence, nor was any deceit in his mouth. Yet it was the Lord's will to crush him and cause him to suffer and though the Lord makes his life a guilt offering, he will see his offspring and prolong his days.

'By his knowledge my righteous servant will justify many, and he will bear their iniquities. He poured out his life unto death and was numbered with the transgressors. For he bore the sin of many and made intercession for the transgressors.' The rabbi noticed something strange. He saw the connection between this man and the Passover sacrifice that his people had performed since the time of Moses. He noticed this man is sacrificed for his people to erase their sins. Which would be blasphemy unless this man was a perfect person which meant he was God himself. No man in himself can be perfect enough to take away sin. This was a spotless lamb, born on Earth, whose father was God himself.

"He then looked at Isaiah's prophecy in chapter 7 verse 14, 'The Lord himself will give you a sign. The virgin will be with child and will give birth to a son and will call him Immanuel.' His next discovery was from Micah 5:2, 'But you, Bethlehem Ephrathah, though you are small among the clans of Judah, out of you will come for me one who will be ruler over Israel, whose origins are from of old, from ancient time.' That one really made him think. He realized that this man would be God incarnate. God wearing flesh. Tying the first coming with the second was this verse in Zechariah 12:10, 'They will look on him, the one they have pierced and mourn for him as one mourns for an only child.' His wife stood by him during his research and when he had verbalized these conclusions she whispered one word,

'Yeshua!' She went out, bought a New Testament, a book that Jews would not even touch, and they read together the four Gospels. The prophecies had been fulfilled. They wept together and pledged their hearts to their Messiah. Of course, he slowly tried to instruct his congregation from the scriptures he could now interpret, but he was rejected. That is when they moved here and bought that house. His wife died shortly after of cancer. She was in your very hospital when she passed. He poured himself into the community, and that is how he dealt with grief I supposed."

"How did he meet you?"

"We were in the corner store together. I was living in a neighborhood close by, and he was shopping. I carried his food home for him, and we visited. I told him of my dream of building a newspaper, and that my father had given me $10,000 to buy a house, but I wanted to put it into a business. That is when he offered for me to live with him, and that I could have his garage to do my printing. I purchased a printer and went to work."

"JON!" They both leapt up and ran to the bedroom to see what had happened to the rabbi.

"I need some coffee!"

Chapter 16

The roads cleared. Jonathan walked home. Rosa and Stephen had a great dinner of roasted chicken and apple pie at Mary's house. Rosa, being bolder than Stephen, asked where they bought their food. Mary told her that they had three freezers, and Todd was a hunter. Not many men had ventured out into the wilderness in the last ten years to hunt, but he had. "I keep a small garden in the spring until late in the summer." Rosa enjoyed the food more than the rest of them. She hadn't had a good meal in a very long time. "We should have been preparing. I just didn't think it would get this bad or last this long." Rosa mumbled with her mouth half full. The children were delightful, but Rosa was riveted by baby Mercy.

When the children were ushered off to bed, the three adults went into the school room. Stephen described step by step his experiments, and Rosa confirmed it by what Grace had done without using her name. They talked about what the results could mean, but their final conclusions were that certain people were immune, and that this was not a contagion. Stephen's blood did react but did not show signs of a full-blown infection.

Mary concluded, "We need further testing. Let's give this some more thought. I'm not comfortable with the results from Stephen's blood. It doesn't make sense to me." Mary concluded the evening and invited Rosa to join them every week. "We need each other to keep our minds from getting off course, and for encouragement's sake."

Over the next two weeks, Stephen was feeling more and more uncomfortable. Mary was back to work after maternity leave and worked part time. He went to see her in the operating room office. He shut the door and whispered. "I've been putting this off, but I think I have a boil on my backside."

"Okay, let's not jump to conclusions. Let me take a look, and I can lance and bandage it for you." She could see his hesitancy. "I do this all this time; I am a great nurse." What could he say? She gave him a gown. "Hop up here, face down." At this point his embarrassment was worse than the boil pain. She quickly sterilized, lanced and bandaged the area. She asked to see his back. She pulled up his shirt and saw the tell-tale sign of crepey skin, a symptom of the plague.

"Stephen, you have it." She somberly put her hand on his shoulder.

"Not, possible, I'm Canadian," he stammered his face turning white.

"Something has changed, this is what you discovered with your experiment. I have no doubts now that this outbreak is not contagious. We tell no one your name, but this is a huge discovery and may change everything we know so far about what we are dealing with." She looked him in the eyes, "Stephen, remember what I told you about going to the Creator who knows the answer to everything? This is the time for you to do it." He stared at her for a few second then dropped to his knees. He begged God for mercy, repented for his sins, promised to live for him.

"Ask Jesus to take over your life and thank him for giving his life to you," Mary added.

After work Mary dropped in on Grace in the ER. She took off her watch and placed it on the desk, Grace followed suit, and they walked outside. "Grace, we have to get a message to the newspaper guy. I heard from Rosa that you know him. One of our foreign workers here at the hospital has a boil and crepey skin. I promised not to say who, and that doesn't matter. I believe we know that this is not contagious, but something is going on. Grace, this could mean other foreigners are coming down with this scourge." Grace promised to pass on the information after work.

She fed the rabbi and left him on the couch with the TV. He looked up at her with a blank look on his face, "They set up kings without my consent; they choose princes without my approval. They sow the wind and reap the whirlwind. The stalk has no head; it will produce no flour. Were it to yield grain, foreigners would swallow it up." He turned toward the TV once again. "I will be back soon. I promise." Grace whispered.

"Tell him I said 'hi.'"

While driving the rabbi's old Chevrolet with barely enough gas for the three miles, she noticed a black car seemed to be following her. She wasn't sure so she passed the house and drove instead to the four drug addicts' home she had visited last fall. The black car with heavily tinted windows drove around and parked on the other side of the road. She knocked and went in. "I'm sorry to...do you remember me? I wonder if I have the wrong house." All four men were sitting at the table eating dinner. "Nope, it's us, clean and sober. What are you doing here?"

"I am being followed by a black car. It is sitting across the street." They peeked through the curtain. "Let's go boys!" They walked over to the car while she stood inside with the door slightly ajar. "She's our nurse checking up on us. Why are you following her?" The car finally left, and she thanked them. "How are you guys so improved?"

"Ask your two doctor friends, the ones who brought us food." They laughed, and she drove off thinking that life was getting crazier and crazier.

She pulled the car into the rabbi's back yard to conceal it then tried the garage door, but it was locked. She knocked on the back door, and Jonathan answered with a dishcloth in his hands. "You aren't supposed to be here." He chided.

"Jonathan, I was followed. That means they are stalking my house. I have something to tell you." He led her to the bedroom and shut the door.

"One of our foreign workers has the plague. Is this an anomaly or is this really happening?"

Jonathan sat on the corner of the mattress. "No, this is the second report I have had about this. It is the confirmation that I needed to be able to put it in my paper; my last one by the way. After tonight, I am going to cover my equipment, hide it behind my junk and leave it be. I have a feeling that change is coming and the heat is going to be turned up. We must lay low for a few weeks. Hopefully by Passover it will be over."

"When is that?"

"It starts on April 11th. Listen, those thugs are probably hassling the rabbi right now. They are not beyond breaking and entering. Throw this over you, it is the rabbi's official robe for ministry." The robe was gray in color and a bit long. "Now walk quickly, and I will follow three blocks behind you. Don't turn around. When you are home and safe, shut your curtains. I will stand outside and wait. He threw on his worker class off-white jumpsuit, and they left. The end of March weather was still very cold, but she felt nothing but fear. The black car was sitting on her street. She ran into the house and into the Rabbi's bedroom. Three men dressed in black wearing blue helmets stood over the rabbi. "What are you doing here? Get out of my house!"

"Who is this man?"

"He is my patient."

"What is wrong with him?"

"Malnutrition, dementia, and he predicts the future." They didn't find her humorous.

"Why is your phone in your bedroom?"

"I am slightly allergic," which was true.

"Why is your television covered up?"

"To keep the dust off," which was not true.

They left, and she closed the curtains. They had riffled through her belongings but had found nothing.

"Are you okay?" she sat on the edge of the rabbi's bed.

"Did you say I was demented, and I predicted the future?"

She smiled, "I was only half lying, Rabbi. Jonathan is going to include in his paper and print tonight that two foreigners now have the plague."

He raised his arms, "Their treasures of silver will be taken over by briers, and thorns will overrun their tents. The days of punishment are coming, the days of reckoning are at hand. Because your sins are so many and your hostility so great. The prophet is considered a fool, the inspired man a maniac." He then drifted off to sleep.

Chapter 17

President Conner was quickly notified that all Pharmakon 6 leaders borrowed from other countries had fled in the middle of the night. They had paid a high price to hire private jets to take them to their respective countries of residence. In these situations, President Conner would usually hold a meeting with congress and maybe even with the generals, but at his first joint session with congress only three attended. He had barely made it himself, so instead he asked his aide for advice.

"I need to go on the 7:00 news and let the people know what has happened, but what did happen? Why would they leave with no notice? I didn't threaten them when they sent me to the hospital. Any idea, Jorge." Jorge did have an idea but needed proof. Jorge knew the deep secrets of the Pharm-6 company, including the murder. The janitor had handed him a bag of the murdered tech's office items that Jorge handed to trusted military police. The name of the victim would soon be revealed. The next newspaper had yet to reach Washington DC, so there might be news he wasn't aware of.

"Sir, let's think about what could have possibly made them leave everything. Maybe a crime?" They were deep in silence for a few minutes.

"What should I tell the public?" The president would have paced the floor but was in so much pain he couldn't.

"You are going to need to replace these leaders with ones with a different focus. I could take your suggestions, do some research and provide a list of possible job replacements. Let the people know that you are working on a new and improved corporation." The president nodded.

"They had become hard to deal with. I think they were running the country more than congress was. What are the head scientists saying about the infection rate?"

"My intel says they think it isn't infectious at all."

"You are kidding me! After all this nonsense about cloaks and separation. Did Pharm-6 know this? I bet they did. I need someone who can do a number on my face, so I am presentable tonight. Any ideas?" The president's adrenalin was pumping.

"Yes, sir, I know an excellent and discrete make-up artist and stylist who can make you look ready to face these new challenges. I will make a few calls."

The president began making notes for his speech, and Jorge quickly called his dad and left a message. "I need that woman's name and number who lives in your neighborhood and does makeup and hair. The president has need of her service. Dad, I also need to know what is in the next edition of the newspaper. Has it come yet? This is important to the future of our country. Can you call around and find out? If you can get a copy, then

I'll take the train to your station and pick it up. I will have to read it in secret. Call me back." He paced the floor for ten minutes. "Hello, yes, this is Jorge. Yes, can you come right away. I will meet you at the train station and walk you into the service entrance to get you a badge. Call me when you are close, Thank you."

"Martha is my name." She was a cheerful black woman in her 50's. She carried a large case and wore high heels.

"Thank you for coming on such short notice. The president is self-conscious, but I assured him that you were discretion itself. I have heard great things about you, so I do trust you. If you pull this off, you may have a permanent job. The president may be needing to make a more public presence now. Pharm-6 fled the country." He whispered the last bit to make sure she knew that it wasn't yet public knowledge.

"Well, that makes sense, I know at least three people, who are working here from Mexico that suddenly came down with boils. They packed up and left in the middle of the night. I think they were worried about ending up in internment camps."

"That's it!" he shouted. "I am so glad I called you. Follow me." After getting a visitors pass, they made their way to the president's office. Jorge knocked loudly.

"Come in, come in." The president seemed to be getting his spirit back.

"Sir, this is Martha. She comes highly recommended, and I think you will find her very enlightening. Martha, tell him what you told me about your three friends." Jorge excused himself and took a call from his father. "Son, I'm driving over with the paper, I figured it would be faster. Let me fill you in on some big news. The editor believes that the plague is now affecting foreigners. Seems they are beginning to flee our country, possibly because they think we are infecting them. The truth is this is not infectious. There are two scientific experiments that have proven this fact. If other countries think that their people are bringing their sickness home with them then they will block the borders. Also, an eyewitness heard plans by the Pharm leader that he ordered the murders of two people for owning this newspaper. I will be there in 20, I need to focus on the road."

"Blazes! What is going on?" Jorge grabbed the satchel from his father, waved goodbye and headed to the White House. He didn't even knock which startled both the president and Martha. "Is there a fire?" the Commander in Chief was almost serious.

"Yes, sir. I have something I want you to read. While Martha trimmed the president's hair, he read the articles and moaned and made remarks like," I can't believe this, I've been a fool, and I am going to get to the bottom of this!" Martha and Jorge gave each other knowing looks. This was the breakthrough the country needed.

"Jorge, we have a week to formulate a new group. You bring them in, and I will interview them. Wait until you hear what is on the news tonight!" A knock on the door and Jorge received a piece of paper. "Sir, I have the name of the office technician and his mother who were murdered by the Pharmacy company." He handed the president the note.

Martha straightened his tie one more time, and he slowly made it to his oval office chair behind the resolute desk. He had never felt so resolute, but the pain pills were wearing off, and he couldn't afford any distractions. He spread out his notes but didn't think he would need them.

"Three, two, one," the cameraman pointed to him, and he began.

"Pharmakon 6 has fled the country. They have murdered a man from their own company and his mother for believing they were insurrectionists. The victims' names are on this slip of paper. I will be notifying their countries to demand that they be extradited and tried for first degree murder. I am already putting together a team that will lead this country into a better and freer future. This pharmacy company withheld information from us, and now I am now officially removing all blockades at statewide borders, and all rules about PPE paraphernalia. Scientists from two different quarters have proven that this is not an infectious disease.

"We will be putting America back together again, and I believe that this plague is now coming to an end. All airlines will deliver, at a discounted price, any foreign peoples wanting to return back to their home countries. The Southern and Northern borders are now open, and your countries will appreciate your return. I am offering this discounted opportunity for two weeks and calling all airlines and military planes to standby for those wanting to depart. We will be keeping you up to date on new information as it comes out. Thank you for your time."

It wasn't a totally truthful report, but it was effectively lifting the spirits of the American people.

Grace was stunned. She had grabbed the rabbi's hand in glee. "I can go visit my mom without getting a pass. Wait, this report isn't totally true, is it? I need that newspaper!"

"Will they not return to Egypt and will not Assyria rule over them because they refuse to repent? Swords will flash in their cities, will destroy the bars of their gates and put an end to their plans," was all the rabbi had to say.

Grace looked through the curtain and was relieved by the absence of the black car. She was hoping for a certain visitor to come by. She gave the rabbi his vitamin drops and helped him get into bed. He took her hand but looked dazed. "They will float away like a twig on the surface of the waters. The high places of wickedness will be destroyed, Sow for yourselves righteousness, reap the fruit of unfailing love, and break up your unplowed ground; for it is time to seek the Lord, until he comes and showers righteousness on you. But you have planted wickedness, you have reaped evil, you have eaten the fruit of deception. Because you have depended on your own strength and on your many warriors, the roar of battle will rise against your people, so that all your fortresses will be devastated. They make many promises, take false oaths and make agreements; therefore, lawsuits spring up like poisonous weeds in a plowed field."

She wondered if the president's promises were false oaths.

Chapter 18

Jonathan did show up at 10:00 pm with a paper under his arm. "I have to leave for work at 5:00 in the morning." Grace complained.

"I am sorry. I just couldn't take any chances."

"Did you hear the speech?"

"Yes, it sounds like he read the paper, but that he told some half-truths to let the foreigners who have just discovered that they are having trouble walking, escape before boils show up on their faces. I think we have just started the journey on the long road home. Now we need this cold weather to go away. It makes me want to flee the country."

"Come stay here again. Are your papers gone?"

"They will be by midnight, then I will lock up and stay low until the peacekeepers leave. I don't think I should stay here; it wouldn't look good, and I may never want to go back home."

"I'll make you some cocoa, I have a little left. The rabbi is tucked into bed. He was in rare form tonight. He was not connected to Earth. I wrote down things he has said lately, here they are."

She jumped up to get cocoa and some leftover cookies to try to delay his departure. She couldn't stand being away from him. She wondered how he felt about her. They talked until 2:00 then he fell asleep on the couch with a blanket thrown over him. When she got up the next morning, he had already gone. "There's food in the fridge, Rabbi. Will you be okay without me?" She was concerned about leaving him alone. He had seemed different, and she wasn't sure he could care for himself. Just then a knock on the door, and Jonathan was back.

"I covered the printing press, hid the ham radio and packed lots of junk around them. I locked up and drove over thinking that the rabbi may need company today."

"Thank you! Try to come up with dinner for tonight. I am going to have to break down and call Lilly for fresh supplies. Bus is coming, got to go."

Rosa was on the bus and wanted to know why Mr. Jonathan's car was out front.

"He is watching the rabbi. How was your week during the blizzard?"

"I had a great time. Stephen and I were snowed in at the hospital, and we became acquainted. He is such a great guy; he is following the One now!"

"The One?"

"He gave himself to God. He is in the family."

"Did he become Catholic?"

"No silly. If you would read your Bible. Jesus said in John that we would be one as he and the Father are one. That means there are no labels. If you add a label, then you are no longer one. Man and wife are one. If you try to label and categorized them, then they become two."

"I guess you are right. I need to start reading the Bible again." She didn't understand anything Rosa had just said. She started her shift. No one had yet to come for face lifts or treatments. What a waste of time.

Jonathan's phone rang. He ran to the bedroom where he had placed what he called "the listening device."

"Hello?" His heart was thumping. He did not like phone calls.

"Hello, my name is Jorge Silva. I am the president's top aide. I tracked down your number through an elaborate network which my father is somewhat a part of. I understand it is your newspaper that the president now has in his possession, "The Zion Herald?" Jonathan nearly fell over. He sat on the bed and answered. "Yes, it is mine."

"The president would like to hire you as the new leader and main newsperson for the Pharmakon 6 company. We will need a new name, of course. Also, I have listed different sectors of this company, and if you can get a paper and pen, I can list them out for you." Jonathan scrambled and with shaky hands gave the okay.

"We need two lab people to run the research and experiment department and someone who is knowledgeable of natural healing and focused on teaching healthy living practices. A technical expert, someone to care for the needs of the underprivileged, and an administrative person who could organize the opening of clinics around the country are vital. We want to start right away with a clinic on the main floor of the old Pharm building.

We are tossing around the idea of a world liaison or at least one who can keep us apprised of the health issues of the world. By the way, we already have the best janitor in town. Jonathan smiled. The president concluded that you would have the greatest network of people to pick from. I have some ideas also, so this isn't all on you. Call me back when you have some names. He would like to start interviewing in three days. I know, it seems rushed, but his next news program is on Tuesday, and he wants to give the people some good news. Call me in the morning with any findings you have, and we can collaborate. By the way, what is your last name?"

Jonathan could barely speak, nor could he think of a single name to add to the president's list. He went to the rabbi and told him what had happened.

"But they did not realize it was I who healed them. I led them with cords of human kindness, with ties of love; I lifted the yoke from their neck and bent down to feed them." The rabbi couldn't help. Jonathan just had to wait until Grace arrived home.

He met her at the door with a hug. She liked that. "What's going on? Is everything alright?"

He let it all spill out while he paced the floor, and while she stood there with her robe and mask still on. The hospital hadn't yet dispensed with the PPE protection.

"Jonathan, this is what we have been waiting and hoping for! The doors are opening. We don't just deal with the crises but also the breakthroughs. This is the bigger things you were meant for. This will be your cup of tea! Do you want one?"

"Want what?"

"A cup of tea." She was in the kitchen already preparing it. "Let's go through the list and see if we know people who would be a good fit for these new positions."

"Two lab people to head research and experiments."

"Stephen Holt, of course. And he may know someone else. Next?" Jonathan jotted down the name.

"Health and welfare people. Natural healing remedies, helping the poor people etc."

"I will ask Rosa if she knows anyone."

"They want to open clinics all over the country, free ones."

"Rosa could help with that."

"And lastly, a tech person is needed. I have no idea about that one."

"We have a start. I will call Rosa and Lily and see if they have any ideas."

Two days later, Rosa, Jonathan, and Grace rode in Stephen's car to Washington DC. Doctors Lily and Chris let the rabbi stay with them. They also offered to start a clinic on the west side of town.

Steven sped through the now removed and piled road blockades, and they cheered. The ride was like water to a thirsty soul. Dressed in their nicest clothes they parked as instructed and met Jorge. He led them up to the White House and into the president's private chamber. Introductions were made, interview questions asked, and the group was hired. They would live in the vacated P-6 condos, their salary was announced, and contracts were signed. The president also gave his okay for a clinic to open in their town. Jorge brought in Nicole Halpin, an expert in natural healing, herbs and oils, and she was also hired.

The president admitted to stretching the truth in his State of the Union Address and explained that it was an important step in cleaning up the P-6 mess as it was now called. No one wanted to say the name of the now debunked company, it was such an embarrassment to the United States. The president wanted to introduce the beginnings of the new team on the news the following night. He had a few more positions to fill and interviews to complete. He was not one to waste time. It was time to prepare for the news report. Jorge stood and the group did too.

Grace noticed the face of the president and whispered, "Martha, he is really suffering, I can see it."

"I know but don't worry, I am getting through to him, and she winked." Grace felt dense, like things were happening around her, that everyone had a secret, and all of it was flying over her head.

The news at 7:00 felt awkward and uncomfortable. They were given two weeks to appear back in Washington DC to begin their new jobs. They made a list while driving home of what they needed to accomplish.

"I think we are getting raises." Rosa announced.

"Especially me!" Jonathan cheered.

Chapter 19

Grace asked the group if they could make a stop in Virginia so she could visit her mom. The surprise on her mom's face made it worth it. "Come in, come in! I saw you on the news last night. I was so shocked. Grace, you didn't tell me anything!"

"It happened so quickly." Just then someone walked in from the kitchen, Grace burst into tears, and gave her brother a giant hug. When they were seated, he began his story. He told of working for a tech giant in San Francisco, but when the company floundered, he worked from home doing piece work for different companies.

"I had the disease so badly that I could barely move, but I still made money. I finally called mom, she prayed with me, and I am feeling so much better." His skin was scarred, and he walked slowly, but it was evident that he was going through a transformation.

Jonathan spoke up, "Do you need a job?" Greg nodded. "The president is looking for a tech guy to run a new company that is being formed. Are you interested?" Greg was thrilled. He dug out his resume, and Jonathan promised to keep him posted. "If you are hired, we will pick you up in two weeks. A condo will be provided so you shouldn't have much to worry about."

Grace's mother walked to the kitchen to bring out snacks for the group, and Jonathan followed her. "Mrs. Iverson, I am very fond of your daughter, and I am planning on proposing to her very soon. I am pretty certain that she will accept, but I wanted to make sure that you had no objections." She was looking like she was going to get emotional. "I think the date will be in the fall as we have so much to do at work for a few months."

"You can have the wedding here. Go look at the back yard, it is big enough. I can take care of everything." Her wheels were spinning. She gave him a hug and carried the tray to the living room. Grace was so happy to see her brother that she didn't notice that her mother was beaming with joy.

They arrived at Lily and Chris's home to pick up the rabbi. The looks on their faces when they answered the door made their hearts sink. "What happened?"

"Your rabbi was rarely coherent and began making no sense. We took him in and did a brain scan. He has a brain tumor. It is large, and we are guessing by his quick decline that it is fast growing. I don't think he has much time." The group was led to the den where the rabbi was asleep on the couch. Grace took his hand and tears blurred her eyes.

"Hello my dear. So glad you are back. I am ready to go home now."

"Which home do you want to go to?"

"The best home, the eternal one."

"Until then, do you want to come back and stay with me?" He nodded his head. "I want you to have a funeral for me while I am still with you. I watched the TV; I know you are leaving. Please do this for me as my way of saying goodbye."

"Are you in pain?"

"But you must return to your God, maintain love and justice and wait for your God always. I will ransom them from the power of the grave; I will redeem them from death. Where, O death, are your plagues? Where, O grave, is your destruction?" He closed his eyes.

The group discussed the idea of a living funeral. No one was for it. They stood in the kitchen so the rabbi couldn't hear the discussion.

"Let's call it a funeral to him, but it will be a celebration of his life and a way of honoring him. I know where I can get flowers. We can have it at my place, so we won't have to move him. It will be just us unless you can think of others we need to invite?" Grace tried to make the conversation more positive.

"He is very fond of the four men that we helped. The ones just a few blocks from where I live." Jonathan inserted.

"Lily, Chris, I accidently ran into them recently. Thank you for taking care of them. It was amazing. Tell us what happened." Grace suddenly remembered her escape from the men in the black car.

"We went over to check on them as you asked, and they were nearly frozen to death and starving. We had brought blankets and food, but the house was miserable. Chris called the electric company, demanded they turn on the electricity and paid them a small fortune to insure it stayed on, then we went to work. It took us eight hours of feeding them, rubbing their feet, and trying to get them warm when finally, we had hot water, and the furnace started warming the place. They were eventually able to move, and Chris bathed each one while I cleaned house. Chris, tell them the rest."

"I carefully peeled off their clothes. We bundled their clothes up in sheets, washed some but ended up tossing the rest. Anyway, I helped them into the tub with baking soda added, and they each soaked for about an hour. While they were in the tub, I pled with each of them to turn away from their hopeless lives. They agreed, I had them pray and repent and accept the Son of God, then I baptized them right there in the bathtub. It was glorious. We came every day to check on them and to bring them supplies. Then after about a week or was it two, we arrived, and there was a note on the table that they had gone to apply for work. Lily and I are dedicated to continuing to help in this way. It was rewarding and the answer to our country's dilemma." Lilly nodded in agreement.

"The president wants healing clinics to be established in the substandard neighborhoods. How would you two like to start one there?" Jonathan suggested.

"We would love that! Also, we packed some boxes for Grace to help with the care of the rabbi. I hope you have room in your trunk?"

Stephen carried the rabbi to the car as he was the strongest of the group. They buckled him in, and he opened his eyes and smiled. They also managed to load the supplies into the trunk.

Stephen dropped everyone off, first Rosa and the other three at Grace's. They carefully brought the old man in and put him to bed, unloaded the trunk and sat down to tea. Grace and Jonathan came up with the order of service for Rabbi's celebration of life and decided that the following Sunday would be the day.

The week of preparations and working at the hospital kept them busy. They gathered in Grace's living room. No one wore black. The rabbi wanted to wear his gray robe, and he held his scriptures against his heart. He was very aware and chose to make a speech.

"Thank you, my friends, for coming." The rabbi glanced around the room and made eye contact with everyone there; the four men from his neighborhood, Grace and Jonathan, Rosa and Stephen, Lily and Chris. "I am a very blessed man to have so many people who love me. This will be a very short speech as I am not sure how much I can say before my brain quits working again. I have a wife and seven children in Heaven. Yes, my wife tried hard to carry her babies, but her body wouldn't allow it. So, since they cannot come to me, I will go to them. I had Grace write out a will for me, and I am giving Jonathan everything I own to do as he pleases with. Here is a bill of sale for my house. I am selling my house to you Jonathan, my name's sake and my friend. Give me a dollar. I hope this will help you not have to pay any death taxes. I lived simply and honestly, I have a clean heart and pure hands. My life belongs to Him."

Everyone then went around the room and talked about how the rabbi had impacted them. He then spoke one last time. "Call me Rabbi Hosea. I will heal their waywardness and love them freely, for my anger has turned away from them. I will be like the dew, and he will blossom like a lily. Like a cedar of Lebanon, he will send down his roots; his young shoots will grow, His splendor will be like an olive tree, his fragrance like a cedar. Men will dwell again in his shade. He will flourish like the grain. He will blossom like a vine, and I will answer him and care for him. Who is wise? He will realize these things. Who is discerning? He will understand them. The ways of the Lord are right; the righteous walk in them, but the rebellious stumble in them." He then closed his eyes and breathed his last.

Chapter 20

President Conner, from his comfortable couch, began an active attack on corruption. He called Russia, China, France and the other countries where the Pharmakon 6 had fled. He reported the murders and told these leaders that he had proof and was going to announce the news on the American television, and that he hoped many countries would be watching. He went on to express his disgust in how his country had trusted these men, housed them and paid them a tremendous salary. They not only broke their contracts, but they committed murder. He could have said more, but what he said had an effect. He wanted the P-6 criminals to be extradited and brought to the United States to be put on trial. None of the leaders agreed to extradition but promised that they would be held accountable in their own countries. The president was pleased.

Martha gave the president a facial and began to prepare him for the nightly news. "There is a small problem that my father mentioned. He has a friend who works in sanitation, and people are starting to toss their robes. Not only are the millions of robes going to cause a landfill problem, but they kill the bacteria that breaks down the trash."

"I see what you mean. That could cause a problem. Isn't there some further use for these garments?"

"You are implementing these crisis centers around the country and if next winter is as bad as this one, maybe people could easily make them into blankets and donate them. The winter robes would be perfect for that. The summer ones could be made into curtains or bedcoverings. All we need is donation spots with containers for robes and people who do the sewing."

"That is a great idea, would you go over to the desk and add that as a note at the bottom of my speech."

He was finally ready for the broadcast. He walked painfully to his desk and carefully sat down. "Thank you for helping me get ready, Martha. The camera men should be here soon," winced the president.

"Sir, if I may, can we have a talk soon about your pain. I do have the best, non-toxic pain killer known to man. It works for nearly everyone, and it may work for you."

"Martha, why have you waited so long! I will have Jorge call you tomorrow to set up a time."

The camera men rolled in and set up. The president did not hold back. He held up a picture of the murdered woman and talked about the corruption in the P-6 company. He apologized that it took so many months into his administration to be able to see what was happening. He reported that he had spoken to heads of countries; that justice had been promised. He ended with the idea of the robes, "Please do not throw them away, they will interfere in the disintegration of garbage in the landfill areas. You will begin to see receptacles where you can donate them for people to sew them into blankets, bedcoverings, curtains or whatever other clever ideas you may have. There will also be receptacles to be able to donate these to our new crisis clinics that are being built across the country. We will not be caught off guard again by a harsh winter."

Jonathan was watching the news with Grace. "You mark my words; businesses will spring up using these materials to make money somehow. Want to take a ride with me?" He now owned the rabbi's old car. He drove through the gate at the doctors' house. "What is this about, Jonathan?" Grace asked.

Lily answered the door, "Come in! There are sandwiches in the den, but first we want to show you where we put Rabbi Hosea's memorial stone." The four walked to the edge of the tree line, and there was a beautifully carved plaque in front of an urn cemented to the ground and sealed. It read, "Rabbi Hosea, Our Help, may he brighten up the Kingdom of Heaven. 1957-2041."

"There are ashes in the urn, but we scattered some around his wife's grave. Did you know that the name *Hosea* is related the names *Joshua* and *Jesus* and means help and salvation? I wonder if he knew that?" Lily added. Jonathan thanked them for taking care of the details after the funeral.

Grace added, "You have no idea how much I appreciate what you have done for him."

"So, they were expecting us?" Grace whispered as they walked to the house. He nodded. Chris was excited about beginning his search for property so they could build the crisis clinic in the old part of town. "I don't like the name crisis clinic, what if someone doesn't think they are having a crisis just a small problem? How about health clinic?"

"No, that sounds like a health spa," Lily asserted.

"We need an uplifting, inviting name for these clinics that the president will approve of."

"Wholeness Clinic?" Grace inputted.

"Sounds new age to me," answered Chris.

"Sick Bay?" They all laughed.

"Clinic for Comfort and Benefit."

"Comfort Clinics of America?"

"Perfect!"

Jonathan pulled out an envelope. I am giving this to you for your clinic. He handed it to Dr. Chris who opened it.

"What's this?"

"I don't need Rabbi Hosea's house; you can turn it into a Comfort Clinic or sell it and build one. I will never live there again and have no use for it, although the garage is full of my junk, so I have less than two weeks to deal with it. I guess I will sell my printing press as my days of insurrection are over." He handed them a house key. "The house is empty of my belongings and most of the Rabbi's. I will let you decide what to do with the rest of it. I'll keep the garage key and hopefully empty it out by the end of the week." Doctors Chris and Lily were thrilled. "We will check it out tomorrow, thank you."

On the way home Grace was quiet. "What's wrong?" Jonathan inquired.

"I am sad that you said that you would never live in that house again."

"We are moving to DC, right?"

"Yes, but not forever. We could work from home. I am going to rent my house to a newly hired nurse and her husband. That way I can keep it and maybe come back someday."

"Good idea, Grace, but I will need a bigger house as I am planning on getting married."

"You are?"

"If you say yes?"

Chapter 21

Jorge called Martha, "I don't know what is going on, but POTUS wants to see you, stat!"

"I am on my way." She tucked a few items into her bag and headed out.

Jorge usher her to the room and shut the door behind him. "I could not wait to get you in here to tell me about your new pain killer. If it works, then we will dispense it at our new Comfort Clinics of America. Do you like the name? Our new newscaster, Jonathan, called it in. I think he is going to be a real asset. Did you see the news report last night? How did I look?" The president was excited and ready for relief.

"Yes, and you looked fabulous, even if I say so myself. And yes, I think you should insist that this new pain killer be used at all the clinics across America. Get comfortable sir, this may take a minute. Are you in a rush or have a meeting?"

He frowned, "No, I have about an hour. Does it take that long to work?"

"Yes, Sir, it does. I want you to listen to me and not interrupt. In fact, lean back and just listen. I am going to read to you for a bit." He frowned some more. "Quit frowning. Hopefully I am about to make your day.

"Sir, Thomas Jefferson, our 3rd president, who drafted and signed the Declaration of Independence from the tyranny of the British Empire wrote this:

'God who gave us life gave us liberty. And can the liberties of a nation be thought secure when we have removed their only firm basis, a conviction in the minds of the people that these liberties are of the Gift of God? That they are not to be violated but with His wrath. Indeed, I tremble for my country when I reflect that God is just; that His justice cannot sleep forever...'

"This excerpt from John Hancock sounds like you, sir, 'Resistance to tyranny becomes the Christian and social duty of each individual...Continue steadfast and, with a proper sense of your dependence on God, nobly defend those rights which heaven gave, and no man ought to take from us.' You are that man, Sir, you have begun to defeat the tyranny that has overcome this country.

"Samuel Adams, the Father of the American Revolution wrote, 'And as it is our duty to extend our wishes to the happiness of the great family of man, I conceive that we cannot better express ourselves that by humbly supplicating the Supreme Ruler of the world that the rod of tyrants may be broken to pieces, and the oppressed made free again; that wars may cease in all the Earth, and that the confusions that are and have been among nations may be overruled by promoting and speedily bringing on that holy and happy period when the kingdom of our Lord and Savior Jesus Christ may be everywhere established, and all people everywhere willingly bow to the scepter of Him who is Prince of Peace.'

"Sir, the only thing coming between you and these beautiful promises is your need to submit to the Kingship of the Heavenly Kingdom, which God desires to extend to Earth. You have yet to submit and if you truly submit, I believe he will heal you and heal this nation because you will finally bring it into its beautiful heavenly alignment. If you refuse, it will only be because you put yourself before the people of this land and that you want your way so you can say you did it your way. How did that work for the last administration? He ruined us and I believe if you went out there, you would see how much we have been ruined. Pray with me sir. Accept the Lordship of Jesus Christ, be washed of your sin. Be humble and accept this message. But you cannot pretend just for the blessing of smooth skin, your heart has to be open to God Almighty as he can see your intent and your thoughts, but He is merciful and will answer your prayers."

The president was quiet for a minute. He knew she was right; his grandmother had said some of these same things to him as a boy. She had told him that he was destined for greatness and would be joined to the founding fathers if he so chose. "I am willing to be willing, Martha, but my heart is cold and dead like a rock. Not sure how to get past it."

She jumped up and laid her hands on him, "Melt his heart, Oh God. Create in him a willingness to submit to having a clean heart. Soften that heart right now. It has a hard rock shell around it, nothing can get in. Sir, I see a cruel father beating you. How can you submit to a Heavenly Father when your earthly father was so evil? He locked you in a closet, you could never do anything right. I see your mother weeping on her death bed, but she is weeping for you. She knows what you suffered, but she felt she had no recourse. I see her dying face and you are standing there begging her not to leave you. Your Heavenly Father says that he has never left you. He saved you from drowning at your favorite water hole when you were ten. He helped you remember answers when you took exams. He gave you favor with the bar exam and pushed you into relationships that furthered your career. You may not have recognized his voice, but he was always encouraging you and prodding you on. Can you hear his voice now?"

They were both emotional, and after about 20 minutes he said he was ready. He prayed a sincere prayer of submission and repentance. He renounced the relationships that brought him destruction, he then forgave his earthly father, releasing him into God's hands. Peace filled the room.

"Quickly, fix my face, I have a meeting in 15 minutes!" They both laughed. The president of the United States of America had a new lease on life.

Chapter 22

The Doctors Lily and Chris loved the little house and decided it would make a perfect clinic. They applied for the grant to get what they needed to get it up and running. The work soon began of clearing out, painting, laying flooring and ordering signs for the front yard and for the entrance. The four friends from down the street came after work to help, and Lily fed them well. Jonathan sold off his equipment and then had a garage sale of what was left of the rabbi's possessions and of his own. Grace wanted to help but now that people weren't fearful of hospitals, the ER was full again. Some broken bones had to be reset, cancer treatments ensued, brain scans, and diagnostics tests were scheduled, it seemed never ending. The hospital vice president even called the two doctors, Lily and Chris, and tried to talk them into coming back. The discussion went back and forth and finally a deal was made. They would schedule their own work hours and have access to hospital equipment for their Comfort Clinic. Their lives just became very busy; they loved it.

Nurses volunteered to work at the clinic one day a week when it opened. The flooring was in, the house was painted, the new furnishings installed, and the signs hung. They ordered phone lines and internet, and by the beginning of June the doors were open.

The new Rapha 7 team logo replaced the P-6 stationary, letter heads and web pages. The new corporation was up and running. Changes were happening so fast that most were working 60 to 80 hours a week.

"Mr. President, I have an updated report from Rapha 7."

"What does Rapha mean again?"

"It means to repair, restore or to make healthful; we can call it R-7 to abbreviate. We have 15 clinics up and running with 75 more in progress. Hospitals are allowing their doctors and nurses to volunteer time to help with the workload. We put out a call for more people to go to nursing school as we have lost thousands of foreign workers in the last few months, although many have stayed on and are applying for citizenship. The general mood of the country is looking up despite the unusual heat so early in the season. As requested, we are beginning the move toward making our own prescription drugs in this country. It will take time, but I agree that it is an important move. All oil drilling and pipelines are in operation, and deals are being made for countries to buy our surplus. Some of it will be given in payment of debt, and the economists are saying that we could be out of debt by the year 2070."

"That's enough good news for today, Jorge, thank you. I have a meeting with the generals. We are getting attacks on our servers at the pentagon. Have the tech guy, Greg, meet us over there. This is the worst attack yet. Pray that we can shut it down."

Greg borrowed a shirt and tie from Jonathan. "I never expected to be called to a meeting with the president." Grace even came downstairs and gave him a big hug. "Go solve the world's problems, big brother." Jorge led him away.

An hour later Grace received a call from Jonathan on her com watch. "Come to my office." His voice was startling, something was wrong. "We need to talk outside," he took his watch off and she did too. They were still suspicious of being spied upon. They rode the elevator to the basement where Joe had his cleaning supplies. Joe was getting ready to start his day.

"Joe, can you spare a minute?"

"Sure boss."

Jonathan pulled a large manilla envelop from his briefcase. "I was putting my office supplies in my desk, but the bottom drawer was sticking; it was rubbing against something. I felt around, and this had been secured to the bottom of the bottom drawer." He pulled out a packet of papers, and the title at the top read, 'Operation Turtledove'. He flipped through the pages so they could see lists of people under longitude and latitude headings.

"What is this?" asked Grace. Joe took the pages and scanned the names, ages and locations of each entry. "These are families. This was not something P-6 did, or I would have known about it. The only other thing it could be, hmmm, remember, at the beginning of the sickness, they took highly infected people to those internment camps? We were told after a few weeks that the gates had been opened, and the people were free to leave, but that most were too sick to move. We assumed that they were still there. But look, here are names of children. These aren't sick people!"

"Who could they be?" Jonathan began pacing. "These people were arrested. But why?"

Joe's eyes widened. "I remember overhearing something that I didn't understand until now. The group before P-6 were talking about the president before James, Wilson, the one that was in office at the beginning of the plague. I heard them mention non-compliant holy rollers. I thought nothing about it, but these people must be the ones who disappeared at the end of December 2030." He looked up with a horrified look on his face, "The government arrested these church folks. We were told a different story on the news, then were told that they had been released."

After Jonathan promised to find out the truth, Joe went to work, and the other two stayed in the basement to come up with a strategy. "I am going to request a meeting with the president. Think about this, most in congress know about this and probably planned it. We cannot let this leak out." Jonathan was livid.

"You cannot tell the president. There are no doubt bugs and listening devices and who know what else, all over the White House. If they are the kind of people that would do this to innocent families, then I can see them sitting at home monitoring everything going on the president's private quarters." Grace whispered.

"True, this is Friday, let's you and I take off tonight, drive home and meet with the doctors. They will help us know what to do."

"I will call and tell them to be expecting us."

They met at a newly opened coffee shop. "It's expensive, but we have coffee again." Dr. Chris announced. They chatted about their personal news, then Jonathan pulled the oversized envelope out of his bag. "Look at what I found hidden under my desk." Lily and Chris looked at the papers for several minutes.

"What does this mean?" Lily was disturbed. Jonathan relayed Joe's theory and Dr. Chris nodded. "This sounds about right. I remember whisperings but took it as gossip. Lily, we can take some time off now, the clinic is running smoothy, and the hospital won't mind. We will GPS these coordinates and visit some of these 400 FEMA camps with a load of supplies. Maybe there are still people there that need help. It has been ten years. The government announced that the doors were open, but that people were too sick to leave. We have to go see for ourselves."

Jonathan also mentioned the possibility of spying going on among some members of congress. "They haven't met together in years, but they could be bugging everything coming out of the White House and our new R-7 group. I am going to hire someone to come in and debug the place." Jonathan handed the file over to the doctors and they promised to keep in touch. Then Jonathan and Grace drove by the clinic.

"It looks wonderful, Rabbi Hosea would be proud. Let's drive by my house, I won't knock, I just want to see it." They parked across the street and sat for a few minutes. "Now look who's being a stalker." Jonathan laughed.

"Let's walk to the park and sit on that bench where we met." Grace was feeling sentimental and was enjoying the cool evening air and the memories. They sat on the bench under the now leafy elm tree. "I want to have 5 or 6 children, Jonathan."

"Where did that come from? These are troubled times, not a good time to bring children into this world," his curt reply fostered an angry response.

"Why not? Our children deserve to live just like you and I deserved to live! How can you say that we can't be trusted enough to bring our family though any crisis that could occur?"

"Think of those families that have been abandoned to FEMA camps for ten years. How did they survive? How are the children? They are probably uneducated, backwards, dirty and hungry. I cannot do that to my children!" Jonathan retorted.

"So, you would tell them that their children shouldn't exist?" The banter was elevating and so was the sound level. Grace jumped up and headed to the car. He followed, but kept talking, "So much grief comes with having children, anything can go wrong."

"What about the grief of a woman who has just been told that she can never have children?"

The ride back to Washington DC was cold and dark, inside the car and outside.

Chapter 23

Quickly, thoroughly and methodically, Lily and Chris packed up the back of their pickup truck. They thought through every scenario. Chris even packed up gifts that he had saved for when he could visit his grandchildren. "I've plotted a circuit to follow. We will travel south weaving from one camp to another, then go north to the ones in Washington State then turn and weave our way to Washington DC to turn in our reports." Lily patted her notebook where she planned on taking copious notes.

"No time to lose, let's go!" Chris was thrilled to be hitting the open road again. Road trips had always been his favorite thing as a kid, and he had missed being able to jump in the car and take off. "Do you have our snacks and drinks?"

"Check!" Chris popped his favorite guitar music into the CD player, and they headed west to cover region 4 on the FEMA camp map. The first one, hidden in the middle of Love Valley, would have been difficult to find without the coordinates. They saw the top of the razor wire before they saw the buildings. After parking the truck, they slowly walked toward the large chain-link gate. Chris carried his bolt cutters. The first thing they saw were two piles of ashes on the ground. As they moved closer, Lily clapped her hand over her mouth and quickly stood behind her husband. "Those are incinerated bodies, Chris," she whispered. He crept closer with her following tightly behind.

"You are right!"

After bravely cutting the chains off the fence, he swung the gate wide open. With eyes scanning the area they crept further and further into the camp. Some of the barrack doors were open, some were shut.

"Hello?" Chris bellowed and Lily nearly fainted, her heart racing.

"Chris, don't shout, you scared me."

"I was already scared," was his reply. Finally, they began to enter the different buildings. "This one is the cafeteria; dirty dishes are still on the table. Something happened. There is food in the refrigerators, but the rats ate the perishables from the cupboards." He opened a freezer. "Look, they still had meat. Let's load these coolers and take it with us." Lily wasn't in favor but complied.

"The people are gone. It looks like suddenly, in the middle of life, poof." observed Lily. Toys were on the ground, clothes were in the washers and dryers, some beds were made, some were not. Chris and Lily covered the entire area taking pictures and taking notes.

"Let's get of here!" Lily whispered and Chris agreed.

They figured that whatever did happen, happened in the morning while some of them were at breakfast, some were still in the barracks, and the children, who had already eaten were outside playing. "What is going on, Chris?"

"I don't know, but I don't believe in alien abduction, so that's ruled out. Take good notes, Lily." They drove several hundred miles to the next camp. Again, using his chain cutters, they entered. They found the same situation except it looked like everyone was in the cafeteria having breakfast. Black stained coffee cups were on the table with bowls crusted over with what could have been oatmeal. This time Chris and Lily raced through the camp to save time and emptied the freezer again. "Notice the train tracks are near the camps. We will probably see this as a pattern. It is how their food arrived. At least there were no scorched bodies at this one."

They toured 7 more camps within three days, staying in cheap motels on the way. In each one they found similar findings. "I'm not sure I want to look at 400 of these creepy ghost towns. This is too much of a mystery for me to deal with. I am ready to go report." Lily was already tired of the adventure. The inns were old, the beds were old and in two of them they found bedbugs and quickly left. "I agree, let's go visit the boys and head to DC." The rest of their trip was more pleasant. Chris's sons were pleased with their new stepmom and the grandkids called her grandma right away which made her very happy. They spent a week with each of them and headed back east.

"There is a camp close by, let's check it out." Lily conceded, and they found a dirt road that led across railroad tracks that led to another chain link fence with razor wire on top that faced inward. Chris cut the chain, and they headed in. This camp looked different. When they walked into the cafeteria a bearded man was sitting at the table eating. He froze and stared and didn't move. The two doctors froze also, "Hello, we are doctors coming to see if you need any help. I have cut the fence so we can take you out of here."

The man burst into tears and sobbed. "I was almost out of food; you came just in time. Let me get cleaned up. I will be right back. Don't go anywhere. Please?" Chris and Lily sat at a table and looked at each other. "We know a few things. First, that none of these gates were opened to the people. Second, that there may be survivors in other camps and third, we can't do this project on our own." Lily then added, "Fourth, we can't trust the government to help."

Clean shaven and donning clean clothes, the thin man appeared carrying a large bulging duffle bag. "My name is Harold Duncan, as in Dunkin Donuts. Do they still exist? I have craved donuts for years. Sorry for the emotional outburst. I didn't think I would ever see another human."

Lily had her notebook out ready to write down information Harold would disclose. She was glad that he had showered because the cab of the pickup seemed tight now that there were three on this journey. Lily explained that they had been on a mission to check out the FEMA camps to see if what the country was told ten years ago was true; that the gates had been opened.

"What else has happened? I am starved not just for donuts, but for information." He laid his head back and shut his eyes while Lily spent the next 2 hours giving the history of the United States. Periodically, tears would slip out the sides of his eyes and roll down his cheeks. He never bothered to wipe them away. She kept her eyes on him through the vizor mirror. She paused, "Now please tell us what happened at your camp. Because what happened at yours seemed to have happened at all of them."

"It was Christmas Eve at the largest church in Houston, during a special midnight service. People drove there with headlights off because, if you remember, church gatherings were outlawed. It was a clear night, and warm. I was a cop hired for security, which seemed funny because the next day I would be arresting them for breaking curfew. I have wondered if they hired me because my Aunt Julie wanted me there to see the production. She had been trying to save my soul for years. The money was good, so I didn't mind.

"The service was nice. The music gave me a nostalgic feeling; I've always loved Christmas. They covered the church windows and kept the lights low, but it didn't work. When we walked out, the military was there with their semi-automatic sniper guns, which didn't make sense to me. These were good people. They loaded us on dozens of buses and delivered us to FEMA camps. They would fill one up, then drive to the next. My aunt was on a different bus, so we weren't together. I imagine other churches in the nation experienced the same treatment. I didn't belong, but it didn't matter; I had been inside the building, so I was guilty. A police badge didn't get me off the hook this time." He paused and took a drink of the iced tea that Lily handed him. "I will never take anything for granted again." he added.

"We were guarded for a while, but then they just left us stranded, with enough food to last maybe one month or two. Pastors took charge and did a pretty good job at maintaining order and keeping us on a schedule. That helped with dealing with depression and hopelessness. We kept expecting the food train to show, but it never did. We were eating breakfast, when suddenly, a blinding light engulfed us. I put my hands over my eyes, and when I opened them. Well, everyone was gone. They had disappeared. I cried for a week and refused to eat. I had missed what my aunt had described as 'the taking out' or 'the catching up.' It was a blessing for her and the others, as we would have slowly starved to death. I had to ration my food then had to set traps for animals or I would have starved. It is interesting that you said the guards were burned up at that other camp. I am not surprised, that light was intense, and I imagine that God wasn't too happy with how they had treated these worshippers."

"So, you think they were taken by God?" Lily asked in disbelief.

"Of course, you didn't think it was aliens, did you?"

Chris pondered, "What do you think about going to the camps between here and DC? I am very concerned about survivors like Harold, considering that he was nearly a goner."

They both agreed that it would be the best thing to do. In all, they visited 42 camps. Harold was the only survivor, but they did find 5 more incinerated bodies. Harold shivered and began praying. "Folks, I have turned over a new leaf because of what I have experienced in the last 10 years. If you need someone to go help visit the camps you missed, then I am your man."

Chapter 24

Late Friday night, Lily, Chris and Harold drove up to the R-7 condos. Jonathan and Grace were waiting for them in the parking lot. Jonathan led Harold to a spare room in his two-bedroom condo. Grace had the doctors go with her. The four talked until 2 am and made plans. First thing in the morning, while the travelers slept, Jonathan called Joe. "I need an exterminator to find the bugs."

Joe was clever and took the hint. "I will call one. Where do you want him sent?" "My condo, as soon as possible."

Lily gave Grace as much meat as her refrigerator would hold, "It was kept in a deep freeze so the meat will still be good. It was wrapped very well." Grace was excited. I will make hors d'oeuvres with some of this for the wedding." Then her face fell, "If we still get married." She relayed the conversation she and Jonathan had over children.

"Making this a matter of prayer is what we need to do. Quit worrying so much, Grace. God is in business of changing hearts." Lily tried to comfort her. Chris jumped up. "Where is the closest donut place." Lily told him, and he ran out.

"Wow, he sure likes donuts." Grace remarked.

Lily laughed, "He promised himself that he would buy Harold donuts today."

The group headed up to Jonathan's condo. Harold jumped up when he saw Chris walk in with the box of donuts. "Wow, you are my new best friend, maybe my only friend as this point." He grabbed a cream filled one with chocolate icing and ate in silence. Lily whispered to Grace, "He's a cop." They giggled.

An hour later there was a knock on the door. He was tall, thin and in his 60's, and he wore a shirt with an exterminator logo on it while carrying a large bag. Jonathan thought perhaps Joe had misunderstood. The man said nothing, but pulled out an electronic device and immediately went to work. The group was stunned but understood and kept quiet. There were bugs in the ceiling lights, the light switches, in every com watch, in the television and the computers. He removed and crushed each one. After a thorough search, he spoke, "My name is Art, and I have never removed so many bugs in one little apartment. You must be important politician." He had an eastern European accent. "I charge $10 per bug, and I think I make small fortune from you." They sent him to Grace's room, and he returned with a handful of smashed devices. "See, I am right."

After sweeping the entire 32 rooms of the R-7 building, it was now time to go to the White House. Jonathan called Jorge, "Hi Jorge, seems we have a bug problem; several hundred have been found and destroyed. I think I should bring the exterminator over to check your rooms. Jorge caught on and agreed. "I'll meet you at the door." Jonathan continued, "After the critters are dealt with, I have someone that you and the president are going to want to meet."

Art fully swept the president's private quarters and his phones, finding 200 bugs. The president was incensed. We have to get to the bottom of this. Jonathan assured him that it would happen.

Then Jonathan took Art to the R-7 office building. "Can I finish tomorrow?" He looked up at the 23 floors. "Today you owe me $5,000. I will meet you here at 5:00 am. It will take all day." Jonathan pulled out his credit card and paid the man.

Jonathan then gathered the group together and took them to the White House. Jorge handed out visitor passes. "This is Harold, he has been locked inside a FEMA camp for 10 years. My two doctor friends visited 42 camps in the last two weeks, and you are not going to believe their story." President Conner was back to his energetic self, which means he didn't really want to sit and listen, but Jonathan assured him that it was a matter of national security. He first told him that he paid Art $5000 to remove 500 bugs, and that hadn't yet included the R-7 office building. "You have a whole lot of spies in your cabinet, Sir. Now here is the story from my two doctor friends." The president listened to their story, then to Harold's. He was riveted, and his mind was going from problem to solution.

"Jorge, your thoughts first." The president still honored his highly intelligent aide.

"Sir, I believe these people were taken by God to save them from dying of starvation. I also believe that if we do not prosecute this heinous crime and remove the culprits, then history will repeat itself."

Jonathan handed the president the manifest that read, 'Operation Turtledove.' "Sir, this was hidden under my desk toward the beginning of the endemic nearly 10 years ago. Whoever is connected to that office, those people will be complicit in this crime."

"Jorge, I am sure you can dig up this information."

"Yes, Sir."

"Let's keep this between us for now, but I agree, we need a team to go to the rest of these camps just in case there are more survivors. Any ideas?"

"We could use the CB and the Ham radio workers who helped me with my newspaper distribution. The organization, headed up by our famous janitor, can hand out coordinates and it could be done quickly," Jonathan offered.

"Do it," accepted the president, "and Jorge, write him a check for $5,000, and give him a blank one for the tomorrow's debugging. I also want a sweep of every room in the Capitol."

Jonathan found Joe vacuuming the fifth floor and they proceeded to the basement. "Joe, I have an assignment. We need our network to gather teams. I want at least 3 people on each team to go to the remaining 358 FEMA camps and with bolt cutters break in and see if there are any survivors. They will have been locked in there for 10 years so they could be dangerous. The teams can salvage anything of worth. I know that the freezers could still contain food. Each group needs at least one policeman or military serviceman. If anyone is found, you may have to take them to a hospital. I trust you on this. I want copious notes taken and reports sent in as soon as each mission has been completed. This is government sanctioned, include my phone number if any team runs into conflict. Do you have any questions?" Joe shook his head, wrapped up the cord and pushed his cart into the storage room.

Chapter 25

President Conner tossed and turned. He was at a loss as to how to flush out the spies in the government. He did not want to be suspicious of everyone in congress, but that is what it was coming to. He was up at 4:00 A.M. drinking his coffee when a plan began to formulate. At 5:00 A.M., he called up Jorge and asked him to bring croissants to his office. Jorge wasn't happy about it and found it an odd request as the president didn't eat pastries. Jorge arrived looking drowsy. "Here you go sir."

"Come on in. There is something I want to run by you to see if you think it will work." He grabbed a pastry, offered one to Jorge, and poured him a cup of coffee. "We must be discreet." Art had sold him a radio wave scrambler, which he turned on. "I don't know who in our administration is bugging every square inch of the government buildings, but today we will find out. We are going to take a walk through the capitol, I am going to loudly tell you that I emailed congress to let them know that I have called a meeting, and we will see how many take the bait. Whoever shows up are the ones using listening devises in the great halls of America." He continued to describe the plan and Jorge nodded and chewed; sometimes asking questions. "Contact the capitol police and have them at full force inside the capitol at exactly 10:15 A.M. ready to arrest anyone who exits. I will already have search warrants available on all congress members in case they are all spies. We could have 535 criminals in that room at one time."

"Surely not, Mr. President!" They left together and rode through the tunnels connecting the White House with the Capitol building. Being early in the morning no one was present. They entered the great hall, and the president began his farce, "I have been the president now for over two years and have yet to have a real State-of-the-Union address. I have sent emails to the congressman calling for a gathering and they must be present for this, or their jobs will be in jeopardy. The days of inactivity while being paid by the government is over. I also called this a special session as I need to report on several implementations that these people need to start deciding on. I am going to cancel the emergency act. It is time to go back to normal.

"When is the meeting sir?" Jorge sounded too loud and too monotone. He was having issues with this playacting.

"I made it for tomorrow morning at 10:00, can you get news cameras ready to record? We may even want this to be live."

"Yes, I can do that." As they walked out Jorge whispered, "Are you sure you want it live?"

"No, but we will record just in case the American people need a wake-up call. This will be a great experiment." They rode together back to the White House and went their separate ways.

The president made a phone call. "Judge, do you have time to meet with me for a few minutes? Can you come to my office?" Judge Ann Croft, a no-nonsense stickler for the law and the constitution sat in the Oval Office in the West Wing of the White House. The president turned on his scrambler. They made small talk for a few minutes. They had not actually met in person. The president assured her that he agreed with her rulings and then went on to tell her the plan he had concocted. He pulled out a plastic bag. "I want to show you this as proof of what I am saying. Here are hundreds of smashed bugging devices that have been found in every quarter of the government buildings. I do not know where they are coming from, but I intend to get to the bottom of this. Would you be willing to help me with this? All I need are search warrants for offices and homes of those who appear at the meeting tomorrow. Their invite will be through these devices." She understood and was just as incensed as he was. She agreed to fax him the proper documents and promised to be at the meeting the following morning. They shook hands and parted company.

Art was combing the office building of the now R-7 pharmacy company, when he received a call. "Art, this is Jonathan, are you available on Tuesday to begin combing through the Capitol building? Art wiped his brow and agreed. "By the way, this building has more bugs than roach farm."

Chapter 26

Representatives Rodger West and his colleague Tina Winters drove together to the capitol building. "I don't know how we missed getting the email from the president. Do you think someone is hacking our computers?" Tina wanted to bite her fingernails, but her mask prohibited the habit she had tried to break for forty years. Some people kept wearing the face coverings despite the change in edicts, it made them feel safe.

"This administration is nothing if not bogus. I don't think he sent a single email and just thought he had. Or his infant aide neglected to do it." Rodger was sneering. "I was tempted to call the others to see if they were aware of the email, but I thought it will be more fun to see heads roll, and then see the president have to apologize."

"Everything is coming down soon. The plan to impeach him, will surely succeed. We have enough evidence to link him to all kinds of illegal activity. Dig deep enough into someone's past, you are sure to find dirt."

"What kind of dirt would they find on you?" He glanced sideways toward her and asked.

She laughed, "I will never tell, plus I have destroyed every shred of evidence, so I am clean as a whistle."

"Well, here we go! Let's go watch the fireworks."

President Conner and Jorge left the White house, the president was excited, his adrenalin pumping. Jorge was terrified, he wondered about the meaning of the word "entrapment." They arrived at the Capitol building at 9:00 which was enough time for Jorge to completely lose his nerve. He used the bathroom 6 times and paced the floor.

"Relax, son, this is what makes life worth living." Jorge shook his head. Finally, a few people filed in, 5, 6, 7. The president kept count and even recognized a few faces. Four men, three women, came in walking very slowly trying not to reveal the tremendous pain that increased with each step. Speaker of the house, majority leaders, dean of the house; all were lifetime politicians, all were old, and all were suffering. The last to come in was number 40. As a congressman would arrive, two pairs of Capitol police were dispatched to begin searching the offices and the homes of each one. Computers were confiscated, and boxes of files were carried out. Secretaries and wide-eyed family members could do nothing but look on. It was a traumatic experience.

President Conner was relieved, he imagined that the whole place would be filled with Criminals. Judge Ann was the last to come in, and the door was shut. The room became a buzz of whispers. Jorge approached the bench, pounded the gavel and announced the president of the United States. No one clapped, stood or even acknowledged the announcement. One man even stood to go. "Sit down senator! I have something to say before you leave." He held up a heavy plastic bag. "Do you see this; these are the hundreds of listening devices that have been uncovered in the government buildings. This building, however, has yet to be debugged." Most of them reached for their cell phones. "You will not be able to use your phones this morning as I have a device that prevents it. As we speak, your offices, and your home offices are being searched. I have the search warrants right here." He held them up. The small crowd squirmed in their seats, then began to scream and shout obscenities. Cameramen who had been filming stepped out of the shadows, which quieted the group, and the president was able to continue.

He talked about Martha, and he read the quotes from the founding fathers that she had given him. He told about his healing, and how it had come from the heart, not from medicine, drugs or anything else. He repeated the oath that he had made to God, to make this nation go back to what the constitution and its writers intended, without modern updates. He rebuked them and hoped that they would also repent. The judge walked out, and the police poured in. The prisoners were taken through the tunnels to solitary confinement in the Washington DC prison cells. They were not allowed phone calls or lawyers. Washington DC did not have the same laws as the rest of the country, and everyone knew it.

That night on the news, the world saw the recording of what had happened that morning. Then the president came on and emphasized what had been said and done earlier. He held up the bag of bugs, he called the nation to repentance and told of the cleansing of his own soul. He had even made the decision to tell the story of the 400 FEMA camps and what was being found in them. "Draw your own conclusions, but I guarantee that the God of Israel will hold those responsible for this great transgression. It seems to me that God himself intervened and saved those families from a most certain death from ten years of incarceration and starvation. Pray with me, "Our Father, which art in Heaven, hallowed be thy name, thy kingdom come, thy will be done, on Earth as it is in Heaven. Give us this day our daily bread and forgive us our debts as we forgive our debtors, and lead us not into temptation, but delivered us from evil; for thine in the kingdom and the power and the glory forever. Amen." President Conner surprised even himself.

"Jorge, it's late, what is going on?" The president slipped on a robe and followed his aide to a meeting room. Jorge whispered, "I am not sure, but NSA is here, and it looks serious. I don't think I am allowed in this meeting."

"It must be serious, usually our appointments are video conferencing meetings."

"I'll wait in the hallway if you need anything, sir." Jorge was nervous; he wondered if the president had made a mistake or worse.

The twelve men stood, and when the president sat down, they sat. "Mr. President, we have been the group assigned to dig into the confiscated files and computers of the men and women who were arrested last month. We have uncovered corruption and have been making more arrests, but we wanted to tell you personally what we have found in certain recordings and emails between Pharmakon 6 and members of congress. It appears, sir, that plans were recorded of Dr. Orillion giving Mr. Dupont instructions to assassinate the vice president after you had won the election. The member of congress shared this information with several contacts, and they were planning on using it to blackmail the doctor. It also appears that the truck exploded after it hit the car. There is evidence that a bomb had been planted on the truck, most likely to cover up their tracks. They didn't want to be blackmailed themselves. I am sorry to bring this news to you so late at night, but we will be making more arrests tomorrow." He slid a paper toward the president who read the list of names and shook his head. "Some of these people were my friends. Why would they want to kill her?"

"We have ascertained that those involved felt like she would have been a hinderance to their global agenda. That is one reason they didn't report it, but also reporting would have exposed their crime of bugging offices. They were just going to sit on it and let it happen. Tribunals will begin tomorrow at Guantanamo Bay; we will keep you notified of our progress." The president stood up and left the room. He whispered to Jorge the crux of the meeting. "I am going to the hospital tomorrow to visit Mae, can you arrange a car at 11:00 in the morning?"

"Yes sir," Jorge replied.

Chapter 27

The midterm elections were on the horizon, and the president called for honest, hardworking citizens to step up and answer the call. He declared that if change was going to happen, it would happen because the people stood together against the evil encroaching the United States.

He had hired Martha as an advisor since he no longer needed make-up. She had a perspective that reached out across the land that DC politicians were blind to. She helped Jorge write some of the president's speeches.

The election was the focus for the next three months. Jonathan was on his own. He compiled the final FEMA reports and had them sent over to the White House, kept the branches of R-7 running smoothly, and his next plan was to expedite American-made medicines. He began preparing the labs and the technicians, had them start with insulin, blood pressure and epilepsy drugs and EpiPens. So much was happening that Jonathan was working 70-80 hours a week.

Grace continued to do research on the world health condition and soon realized that almost every country was in a crisis with the boils and the 'melting skin' as some called it. Only 20% of Africa was infected, China 30%, India 60%, but Europe, including Scandinavia was close to 90%. They had learned what not to do from watching the United States. Grace realized that what she cared about was the world and felt she wasn't accomplishing much. She also realized that she no longer wanted to be married to a man who was married to his career and who would not give her children. She didn't have a ring to return because she had never received one. She handed in her resignation to the president by fax, and disposed of everything that wouldn't fit into her two suitcases. She cleared personal items from her office and left her com phone on her desk, then she took the train to Virginia.

Grace's mom drove the thirty minutes and picked her up at end of the metro station's orange line. Her mom knew enough to not ask questions; she would keep quiet until Grace decided to begin the conversation. Jonathan didn't miss her for a week, he didn't even know that she had quit. When he did figure it out, he went to Rosa who just shrugged and said that Grace had quit her job. Jonathan knew he was in trouble, so he confided in Dr. Chris. "Did Grace go back to North Carolina?"

"No, I haven't seen her. I image she must have gone to her mom's. What happened?"

"I don't know. She just quit, packed up and left; didn't even leave a note. Hold on I have a call." Chris was on hold for 10 minutes then finally hung up.

"Lily, I think Washington DC has interfered with Jonathan and Grace's wedding plans. She has disappeared, and I think I know why."

"That's too bad, let's drive up to her mom's house in a few weeks and see how she is doing."

"How do you know she is there?"

"That's where I would have gone."

The election wars were raging in full force, but it wasn't really a war, but more of a surrender. Good, honest people running against good, honest people. Picking the best one was going to be the difficult part. The president refused to endorse anyone unless it was someone running against lifers from the old slimy regime.

Eventually, when all the reports were in, the president gave the final report on the FEMA camp debacle. He gave details about what was found; 10 people were still alive, and several charred bodies were found on the outside of the premises. The president made the report that night on the news. He told about the manifesto and where it had been hidden and about the names of the detainees that had been listed. He told the people that he knew some of their relatives and family members had never come home, but he would post the pages of names and of the 10 survivors online to give finality to the situation. He apologized on behalf of the overreaching power and control of the government that had caused such misery and promised that he would do all he could to bring back the freedoms and rights the Constitution had afforded the American citizens.

On a brighter note, he announced the need for journalists to step up and begin reporting and researching. He added that a position had opened for research within his administration and that resumes would be accepted for the next two weeks.

Jonathan watched the news and shook his head. He was distracted and angry about Grace leaving without a word. He hadn't done anything or said anything wrong, well, since the argument about having children. He slapped his leg, rose, and went back to work.

Trials were also on the menu for the Month of July and August. There was so much evidence against the 40 traitors that even plea deals were put to rest. Some of them gave names, spoke of blackmail and played the victim. This only gave more for the investigators to dig into. The entire web of deviousness extended to senators, governors, judges, mayors, chief of police and then to other countries' leaders. Spying was widespread and dirty; the honest heads of countries began the hunt too.

Grace talked to her mom about an idea that she had. "I think we need to send teams to other countries, an extension of our Comfort Clinics. We have an opportunity, now that the world sees that we have largely pulled out of the mess, to pass on what we've learned."

"I think that is a great idea, but haven't you burned your bridges, your connections?"

Grace hung her head. "I'll go tomorrow and apply at the hospital down the road, maybe they need a nurse." She did get a job as an operating room nurse at top pay. She enjoyed keeping busy and worked long hours. Her October birthday came and went and only Rosa reached out to her.

"Happy Birthday! How are you doing?" Grace forced herself to sound cheerful as she described her new job. "How's everything at R-7?"

"Busy! The pharmacy production is increasing so the company is expanding. It is starting to purchase the smaller pharmacies around the country focusing only on life saving medicines. We aren't interested in the non-essentials. You are probably watching the news reports, so you are seeing that things are cleaning up. Stephen is talking about moving to one of the smaller companies to help with the takeover. He's asked me to come with him. I know this is a sore spot, but he's asked me to marry him. We are going to go before a justice of the peace in two weeks. I really, really want you to be there?"

"Of course, Rosa, I would be honored. What color should I wear? Can I bring the flowers?"

Grace took the metro in a lavender dress that went just below the knees. Her camel-colored coat hid the dress but not the lovely hairdo. Her mother had pulled it back with sparkly clips and let the rest flow down to the middle of her back. She was careful to not put on too much make-up, and was glad, people were already looking at her or was it at the bouquet of white roses.

Chapter 28

Rosa was standing in front of the courthouse dressed in a pale purple satin dress than went just below the knee, a short veil caught a breeze and flew up in the back as she nervously rocked back and forth on satin white high heels. Grace jumped out of the ride share car, bound delicately up the steps and hugged her best friend.

"The roses are perfect! Did you do the purple ribbon yourself?" Rosa seemed nervous.

"I sure did, I'm getting good, huh?" She stopped and was no longer smiling. Jonathan walked up the sidewalk, and their eyes met. "You did not tell me that he would be here!"

"What was I to do, Grace? He was Stephen's choice, and I knew you wouldn't come if I told you." They turned and walked into the courthouse. Grace did not want to ruin this celebration so decided to grin and bear it until she could run away again. The ceremony was over quickly, and Rosa and Stephen said their goodbyes. Grace put on her coat and immediately began calling for a ride when Jonathan took the phone from her and shut it off. "Let me take you home, please?" Grace wouldn't look at him. "I just want time to tell you how sorry I am for being so neglectful, and being an idiot, and for losing the only thing in life that had meaning. Grace, please, if for no other reason, let me be forgiven." Grace, being a mercy person agreed. They walked to the parking garage without speaking. The sun was going down in the early autumn sky. Grace kept her face towards the window and away from him.

She realized that he wasn't taking her home but took a right turn instead of turning left. "Where are we going?"

"I thought maybe you wouldn't mind getting something to eat." He drove down a long driveway to an old mansion with a restaurant sign out front. He opened the door for her, and they walked up the steps. "Reservation for two for Jonathan Friedman." She clinched her teeth; *how dare he assume I would want to go out with him.* With furrowed brow she followed him inside. A small table in a private corner was set up with a beautiful bouquet of red roses, a bottle of wine and a box of her favorite chocolates.

"Please don't be angry with me. I talked to Dr. Chris, and he told me that I was dealing with a fear of failure, and that is why I dug into my work like a crazy fool. I never felt like a success, and this was the best shot I would ever have. Then when Chris asked if you had returned my ring, I realized how much you had to be offended about. He told me that fear keeps good things from happening, and one day you wake up an old man with nothing. I thought of the book, *The Christmas Carol*, and saw myself as a miserable old rich guy with no family or friends." He handed her an envelope; it was a Valentine's Day card. "I really want to make it up to you." She opened the card and shiny hearts fell out. It read, "Happy Valentine's Day to the only girl I have ever loved." At the bottom he wrote, "I want to have 6 children with you so do you think we could get married?" She looked up, and he had knelt down and had opened a small box. It was a sapphire surrounded by small diamonds. "Will you be my wife? If it helps, I quit my office job."

"Yes, I will. But where is home now?"

Grace's mother met them at the door and gave them both a hug, "My prayers are answered!" I made up a bed in the guest room, Jonathan. Good-night you two." They talked until early morning. He told her that Martha, the president's advisor took over his job as reporter for R-7, and that he could now work from home as a journalist.

Grace shared her idea about sending teams into the countries that needed help with the plague, to bring them the answers they needed. Jonathan took notes and decided to write out a proposal to the President. "We could be the first team to go to a few countries. I could then report on what we are doing to give others a vision. We should take someone with us who can talk about their personal recovery story."

"Where are we going to live? Grace asked again.

"It's your choice," He answered.

"I want to go back to my home on Hospital Lane. My tenants are moving out, and I miss it."

"Can we plan a wedding in a week?" He asked.

"How about two?"

On October 30th, Grace and Jonathan said their vows on a sunny but chilly day in the backyard of Mrs. Iverson's house. Grace borrowed Lily's wedding dress and Rosa, as the matron of honor, wore her own wedding dress. Grace carried one lavender rose and wore her mother's veil. They went inside for cake and toasts from Stephen, Dr. Chris and Greg. Then Jonathan presented his plan to go into the countries that were struggling. "If we have a heart that cares, then we will teach what we took thirteen years to discover. If the president will present this idea and a hundred people step up, then we can reach out to the whole world in just a few years. What do you think?"

Mary and Todd were there with their children, and she was the first to speak up, "This is an odd but wonderful wedding topic and a great idea. Maybe have people sign up for the country or countries they wish to visit? Todd and I pick Belize and Panama, both places we have been and are comfortable taking our children to."

"Stephen and I will go to Brazil, Ecuador and Chili, but maybe not all in one trip."

"Lily and I will go where no one else choses. We can easily take a week each month to travel."

Jonathan spoke up. "I will need someone who can contact heads of state in each country and set up meetings. We will let the country itself decide where the venues will be held, how it is broadcast, and we will also insist that the government officials attend. We can reach the people, but to avoid the tyranny, we need to reach the leaders. Larger countries will need more than one team. We need to include small villages with no outside contact. I want at least 3 people on a team with one who has come out of the crisis with a story. We also need to interview those we do not know to make sure we are on the same page." Rosa raised her hand. "I would like to be a part of this in whatever capacity is needed."

"The next step is to convince Mr. President."

Grace and Jonathan moved back into Grace's home, and she worked part time at the hospital and was happy to be there. She visited Cindy on a Saturday while Jonathan was in Washington. "Hello, I am here to visit Cindy?" She did not recognize the girl.

"I'm Cindy, who are you?" Putting voices with faces took some getting used to. When the young girl realized who Grace was, she hugged her tight and invited her to come in. "I have a baby brother, Chad, come see. Cindy grabbed her hand and took her to the nursery where Cindy's mom, Sonja, was patting a baby's back. Grace felt the old pang come back. They went back and sat on the couch and soon Sonja joined them. Grace talked about her wedding and talked about the teams that were going to go around the world to help the other countries understand how to pull out of the plague. "Mom, can I go?" Cindy begged. "I'm almost 16!"

"Cindy could go with us. We are looking for someone who would tell their plague story of healing. We are going to Japan and Guam. An interpreter is hired. We will only be there a week."

"I will talk to your father about it, but it does sound like the perfect adventure, one that serves God and people."

Jonathan, sitting next to the president, went on the nightly news to make an appeal to the American people to volunteer to go and speak to countries on how to come out of the endemic. Jonathan explained the ground rules and gave the email address to the forms that needed to be filled out. At the bottom of the page was a place to write the names of additional people who desire to be on a team. Pastors and missionaries who were forced to leave their mission fields were encouraged to get involved. On the form was a place for a summary of their personal story.

Within the week nearly fifty thousand people had filled out the forms. Jonathan was ecstatic. He called a meeting at Lily and Chris's home that included Todd and Mary, Stephen and Rosa. They spent hours organizing the data on the countries and the teams. Rosa sorted the information into the computer, and they made copies.

"I see some familiar names on this list." Jonathan noticed, "Here's Joe, Herb and Harold, and isn't this a Supreme Court Judge?" They saw pastors' names, and those of people who were running for office in the next election. "If these teams serve two, or three countries, we will have covered the globe in a matter of a few months. We are counting on each country broadcasting these meetings from their local stations. Sorry honey, I am going to be busy for a few months getting this organized." Chris and Lily also offered their services. Lily added, "Let's call this 'Three Months of Harvest.'" They agreed.

The project was slated to begin after the midterm elections. The teams were notified and given the dates and places of the meetings that had been set up by Rosa and Jonathan. They were told to speak from their hearts and to trust God for the rest. They were to tell their stories, lead the people in repentance, and encourage the churches. Countries that were already broadcasting the U.S. nightly news were eliminated from the list. A few other countries would not allow the teams to enter, and some, it was discovered, were doing just fine, and even better than the United States. Brazil was crossed off the list, "They are praying for us!" Rosa cheered.

Harold and Cindy stood at the gate with Jonathan and Grace getting ready to board. They had read the handout about the culture and manners of the places they were visiting. Cindy had practiced her speech leaving out the part about her grandmother but adding that she had been a rebellious teenager. Harold would tell the story of the FEMA camps and being deserted by the government and how he had realized that he was left behind because he did not believe in God at the time. He had prayed and repented and after ten years, at the point of starvation, a couple came to rescue him.

The Japanese government was polite and listened to the messages of the three people in an office building. They wore masks, but it did not hide the gruesome effects of the plague. Grace ended with talking about the two crucial experiments, hers and Stephen's and how they both proved that this was not an infectious disease, it was a disease from the soul of man who had rejected their Creator. The quiet men bowed their heads, prayed silently, then the president agreed to let the 4 of them speak to the country that night on the news. It was a thrilling experience.

Chapter 29

The midterm elections on that second Tuesday of November 2042 were historic. The new politicians won by a landslide, and many of the old ones were made to retire. That night President Conner congratulated and welcomed the new members of congress reading the names of each one. He presented his idea of bringing an easy IRS form to the country. Everyone would pay 9% of earnings starting at age 18, or 20 if they were college students. He added that the IRS had lost so many employees that this would cut the need for finding new ones. The 9% that he came up with was because, "If God was asking for 10%, then the government did not deserve more than that." He talked about how the economic turnaround could be achieved, but that it would take years. He hoped that with the blessing of Providence, they could do it before the end of his second term. He called for prison reform among the new lawmakers, and answers to homelessness and suicides. "We can help other countries, but we need to solve our own serious problems. I want to mention a bill that is before the House right now. It is a bill that puts the people back into 'We the people.' So many in congress have been bought, cajoled, and even blackmailed for the purpose of serving a political agenda that is not for the people but for padding pockets of the elite. Two points in this that I want to present, the first gives you, the people, the right to vote on every bill that is coming before the Senate. Before each opportunity to vote, we will have a formal debate on the topic so that you can see both sides of the issue. Interested people who watch these debates are then given the opportunity to log on and help decide the future of this country. The Supreme Court debates will also be broadcast, and the people will have the tenth vote in those decisions. Have hope again and God bless."

Jonathan watched the news report and even though he was encouraged, he had a gnawing uncomfortable feeling in his gut. "Grace, have we really neglected our own people while reaching the world?" He began formulating a plan for reaching the prisons. "Jorge, I need you to relay a message to the president. I know he's busy, but I have come up with a plan to go into prisons. I just need him to talk to the Federal Bureau of Prisons to allow teams to come in and assist in the well-being of the inmates. Then just have him ask for volunteers on the 7:00 news. Those willing to serve can fill out the same online forms. We are going to reach every prison within three months, Jorge, this is going to be good." President Conner, always with an open mind, went ahead and contacted the BOP, the Federal Bureau of Prisons, and then gave the announcement on the news that night. The following day hundreds of forms came in, and the group began to organize this new project.

Harold gave Jonathan a call the next day, "I think I would rather be involved in prison visits than go to foreign countries. I know what prison is like, and I have a great story for this." Jonathan put him in charge of the whole operation.

The first official visit found six brave men entering the Louisiana State Penitentiary, or the "Alcatraz of the South", its nickname. Its 7,000 prisoners were only watched and cared by 800 staff members, cut in less than half by the plague. The prison's history was gruesome and cruel. Harold wished he had not read the information. They prayed silently then were given access to the sound system connected to the warden's office. The warden was never seen during the visit, but a young officer watched over the group.

"My name is Harold Duncan. I want to tell you about my ten-year solitary confinement in a FEMA camp." He continued his story then told of his redemption. "Search your hearts, decide if you have enough hope for healing, not of your body but of your soul. I am going to read you a message while you are deciding. 'Surely the arm of the Lord is not too short to save, nor his ear too dull to hear. But your iniquities have separated you from you God; your sins have hidden his face from you. We look for light, but all is darkness; for brightness, but we walk in deep shadows. Like the blind we grope along the wall, feeling our way like men without eyes. At midday we stumble as if it were twilight; among the strong we are like the dead. We all growl like bears; we moan mournfully like doves. We look for deliverance, but it is far away. For our offenses are many in your sight, and our sins testify against us. Our offenses are ever with us.

We acknowledge our iniquities, rebellion and treachery against the Lord, turning our backs on our God, fomenting oppression and revolt.' If this describes you and you are ready for a new chapter in your life, then we will be coming to your cells to meet with each of you over the next two weeks."

Harold looked at the young guard who was blowing his nose. "If you can help these men then God bless you." They split into three groups and began going into the cells. Doors were not closed or locked, "It is because they are too sick to move. We must serve their food to them in bed. We do not have the nursing staff needed to take care of this misery." The guard left them to do their work.

The prison smelled like death, Harold and Dr. Chris walked into the first cell. Two men in a bunk bed barely turned their heads. Their clothes were stuck to their bodies, and their faces were so swollen that their identities would have been difficult to determine. Harold tried hard not to gag. He introduced himself and tried to impart hope to the men. "Can you repent now for your sins? Can you make Him Lord of your life? Can we pray for you?" The man, through blistered and puffy lips said yes. So, they prayed. Dr. Chris had an idea and took water and sprinkled it of the men's bodies as sort of a modified baptism. Tears flowed.

After eight hours only twenty-four men were visited. As they walked out of the prison, the enormity of the project hit them. "I'm going to call Jonathan," Chris declared

"Chris, how did it go today?" The doctor used as many adjectives as he could come up with to emphasize the misery and hopelessness that they had encountered. "We cannot just pray for them; they are a stinking foul mess and in need of clean clothes and good food. Hell could not possibly be worse. In 8 hours, we only covered 24 men, and there are 7,000 in total! This will take us months. Yes, they did pray with us, I even sprinkled water on them. But this is a long-term project that will include health care workers, cooks and teachers."

"I am on this, Chris. Keep going and we will get this done together. I will let you know when I come up with a plan." Jonathan was home with Grace, and she overheard the conversation. Dr. Chris had a loud voice. "We need to have something good for them by Christmas, but right now I think the president needs to call for people in the area to volunteer in the laundry area and the kitchen. We need to get med beds in there also, and janitors." Grace was good at brainstorming.

"Jorge? Me again. I am sorry to bother you. Are you with the president? Can you put me on speaker phone?"

"Jonathan! We are missing you around here, but Martha is getting very popular as our newscaster. What is going on?"

Jonathan copied the same adjectives that the doctor had used then presented Grace's solution. This would be the test of the heart of the president.

"I will announce it tonight calling for people in the area to bring their buckets and rubber gloves. I will call on hospitals to truck in their med beds until we have treated every man in there. I will describe the need for food and cooks, and we will see what happens. It also sounds like you could use about 300 more teams, so watch your emails. I expect help will pour in. You are doing a great work, son. Thank you."

Rosa was contacted and she and her team organized the workers. The warden was contacted to alert him to the clean-up project that would be ensuing. The Warden never showed his face, but it was assumed that he was watching the project from his private room though CCTV. Two days later 20 med beds arrived and were set up in the cafeteria. Nurses volunteered to bath the men for 20 days, an hour per prisoner. Women arrived and kept the prison washers and dryers running continuously. Janitors arrived and mopped and scrubbed floors, walls, and toilets. Doctors arrived, gave checkups, and ordered antibiotics for secondary infections. Dentists came and offered their services. Hams, sweet potatoes and pies were prepared for the men for their Thanksgiving dinner. By Christmas, the med beds were gone and there was a celebration in the cafeteria. Harold opened with prayer and with verses, "Arise, shine, for your light has come, and the glory of the Lord rises upon you. See, darkness covers the earth and thick darkness is over the peoples, but the Lord rises upon you and his glory appears over you. Lift your eyes and look about you; All assemble and come to you!"

He spoke of their importance; how God had a purpose and plan for each of them, and that it was never too late to start over. Harold again made a call for repentance. More men prayed for forgiveness and for help to live for God. Every person, cook, janitor, doctor, nurse and team member scattered and prayed with every one of the 2,000 men in the lunchroom. They had eaten in three shifts; it had taken an hour to get each group to their seats, as some had barely walked in years. Pain pills had made the party possible.

Harold again spoke. "Would anyone here like to share what these last two months have meant to them?" An older man raised his hand and slowly stood up, "I speak for all of us, we are very thankful for your help, and I swear to you that we are changed men and will be good people and love God." The entire room of prisoners rose to their feet in agreement.

Chapter 30

"It took 3 months to transform the prison in Louisiana. How are we going to reach the 12 largest prisons in the country in the next 3 months?" Jonathan again was talking to the president in his quarters in Washington DC. It was January and the three-month plan for the world was in full swing. Thousands of missionaries went back to their countries where they had served. The goal of reaching one hundred nations in ninety days looked like it would be reachable. The prisons were another story. The president responded, "Let me make some calls. I have some ideas. They are way out there but nothing ventured, nothing gained as they say. I'll be in touch, Jonathan."

Jonathan drove the five hours home and arrived late in the day. Grace had a nice dinner on the table and seemed to be in a good mood. They were enjoying their meal when Grace pulled out a few pictures. "I want to show you something." She handed him pictures that made no sense to him. "Is this from the hospital?" He asked.

"Yes, it is called an ultrasound picture. It shows two little people growing who will be calling you Daddy!"

"Twins?"

Grace had to quit her job by the end of February and had to stay off her feet. She worked instead for the 'Thirty Days of Harvest." She read reports and compiled the information and forwarded it to the team and to the president. President Conner's idea for the remaining prisons was brilliant. The men from the first Louisiana prison who healed up and went to Bible classes were then propelled into ministry to the next prison on the list and served as janitors, laundry workers, and kitchens helpers. Nurses' assistants helped the men get down the stairs into the twenty med beds that now moved from prison to prison. Men and women were committed to seeing the entire project to its completion even if it took a year. After the large prisons, they intended on visiting the smaller ones and the jails.

Reports flooded in from all corners of the Earth, nearly a billion people had been reached, and that was only the ones they knew about. By the end of March each country had seen the kingdom being built and pastors and ministers took over the process. Fear had been crushed, and most of the Earth breathed free again. Those countries whose leaders refused had a remarkable underground movement. It was a glorious time that had never occurred before in the history of mankind.

Drs. Lily and Chris celebrated by hosting a get together at their home. Rosa and Steven picked up Cindy, the others were Harold, Greg, Mary, Todd, Jonathan and Grace. They talked into the night sharing stories and victories. Harold was asked why he had chosen such an odd scripture to read at his first prison. "It was in a dream I had. And I use it every time I was handed the microphone." They laughed. Grace spoke up, "I am having twin boys, and we are going to name them Joel and Amos, after Hosea!" Stephen looked up quizzically. "It's because Joel and Amos come after Hosea in the Bible." She answered his look, and they all laughed. Mary brought up her move in starting a Classical Christian Homeschool Community that was growing quickly. "We have six subjects, and we meet once a week. All the other days the students work from home. We teach Latin, logic, math, literature and composition, science and history. I thought you may want to prepare now for the future, Grace!"

The guests left and Jonathan and Grace had prepared to spend the night.

"Lily, you, Rosa and Mary will deliver my babies, right?"

"Stop worrying. We have arranged to stay here in town and not go anywhere for the next four months."

"I wish Jonathan would make the same commitment."

"One of us will come and stay with you if he leaves. Our faith is always tested, Grace. Jesus wants to know that when he comes back to Earth will he find faith in you?"

"You are right, of course."

The two doctors stood as if to make an announcement. "Lily and I have something we want to propose to you both. Give it some thought if you need to. We spend most of our time traveling the world, visiting grandkids and working the clinic. We are never home. We were wondering if you and Grace would agree to exchanging houses with us. You are going to need more room, especially when your mother comes to help you with the twins.

And we would like to be closer to the clinic and the hospital. We would still pay the gardener, and you could cover utilities. What do you think?"

"We don't know what to say. That is so generous!" Jonathan managed.

"We would love that!" Grace added.

"Good, you can move in right after the babies are born. It is settled."

By Passover that year, the prison project was completed. Many of the prisoners became leaders in the prison community, and when they were up for parole, were easily discharged. The warden from the first prison sent a long letter of commendation to those that had intervened in his facility. He added that because of it, he was a changed man and wrote an interesting verse at the bottom of the page. "Some sat in darkness and the deepest gloom, prisoners suffering in iron chains, for they had rebelled against the words of God, so he subjected them to bitter labor. Then they cried to the Lord in their trouble, He brought them out of darkness and the deepest gloom and broke away their chains. Let them give thanks to the Lord for his unfailing love and his wonderful deeds for men, for he breaks down gates of bronze and cuts through bars of iron. Psalm 107:10-16."

Grace couldn't leave the house and was miserable. Jonathan didn't leave very often and worked at trying to keep her comfortable. The weather turned hot in May and Grace couldn't keep cool. "This is August weather, can you turn up the air conditioning, please?"

Many states had to ration water because of drought. There were water wars between a few states that became bitter. Crops were failing and cattle were dying. Then the fires begin to spread. Church leaders called for a nationwide forty days of fasting and prayer. The food trains couldn't run because of record heat.

Martha, from the White House, reported on the dire condition of the country, then reported on the severe floods occurring in several countries on the other side of the world. "The President of the United States is calling for a three day fast to call on God to send rain and end the heat wave."

"If May is like this, what are we going to do in three months?" Jonathan had enough to worry about dealing with keeping a very pregnant wife happy. That night his troubled dreams took him down dark paths. He couldn't find one with light. He ran but wasn't going anywhere. Around a dark corner stood the rabbi smiling at him and clapping his hands. Jonathan was irritated at the man's cheerfulness when he was filled with fear. The rabbi spoke, "No shred of dread or intimidation. No cowardice or oppression. No chokehold of fear or insecurity, just grasp the large pillow of hope." He woke with a start and laughed, "That sounds like the rabbi."

"Jonathan! It's time!" They drove the three miles to the hospital and Mary, Lily and Rosa soon followed. They had the entire third floor birthing center and nursery to themselves, and after twelve hours, they had two perfect baby boys. Grandma soon arrived and a week later the family moved into a very impressive mansion, complete with grand piano and food larder that made the suffering of the last ten years seem like a forgotten nightmare.

A month went by, and the heat wave broke 140 degrees in some areas. People moved north to the Dakotas, Wisconsin and Minnesota. Lily called Jonathan on July first, "Jonathan, we need help. People in the neighborhood do not have air conditioning. We are losing some of the elderly. Do you think you would mind taking in a few people until this passes over?"

"Sure, how many are we talking about?"

"Thirty."

After a pause, "Hold on, let me talk to Grace."

"She says yes. I'll get the basement prepared. It is about 20 degrees cooler down there. See you soon."

"I'm going to load them in the pickup after dark. We are in a desperate situation here. Thank you!"

Chapter 31

September arrived, rain did not. Black circles were evident under Grace's eyes. "I need to get out of the house, Jonathan! I am not used to living with this many people around. I feel trapped and confined to my room."

"Let's plan a Rosh Hashanah celebration for September 22nd. We can have songs and prayers and a feast. The rabbi gave me his shofar, I need to practice, but it will be fun."

Grace rolled her eyes, "Sounds like fun, Joel is crying would you get him for me? And could you bring me my phone?"

"Hi, Rosa, how are you doing? Want to come over and hold a baby or two? Just kidding, but Jonathan is planning a party on the 22nd, I'm hoping you can come? Yes, how did you know about Rosh Hashana?"

The pool table had been removed from the large room, and it was filled with people. The old friends and the new ones were there, most sitting on the floor. Jonathan took charge and lead the group in some old choruses that if they didn't know, were easy to learn. He then made a speech that was very much like a sermon.

"We have been weary souls in the last twelve years, but now it is time to rejoice. This is not a time for cynicism or negative self-talk, but a time to be grateful. It is a time to be energetic having goals and dreams. This is not a time to be impatient with others or give up enjoying our relationships with one another. God has called each of you and whatever it is that he has for you, it will fill you with joy and fulfillment." He then took the shofar and blew long and loud several times. Grace and Rosa covered the babies' ears. At that moment a flash of light went overhead and in a split second the room was empty.

Scripture References
Hosea 4:1-3; 5:13-15; 6:1-3; 7:13-14; 8:4,7; 9:7; 10:4,12-13; 11:3-4; 12:6; 14:4-6,9
Isaiah 59
Isaiah 60:1-4

Made in the USA
Middletown, DE
14 January 2025

68601957R00124